HER OUTBACK RESCUER

BY

MARION LENNOX

First published in Great Britain 2012
by Mills & Boon, an imprint of Harlequin (UK) Limited.
Large Print edition 2012
Harlequin (UK) Limited, Eton House,
18-24 Paradise Road, Richmond, Surrey TW9 1SR

© Marion Lennox 2012

ISBN: 978 0 263 22637 9

Printed and bound in Great Britain
by CPI Antony Rowe, Chippenham, Wiltshire

For Elizabeth and for Mary Michele.

*Without your friendship, laughter and belief,
my stories would never happen.*

I love you both.

CHAPTER ONE

THE Structure and History of Granite looked fascinating reading. He could scarcely imagine the plot.

But plots weren't on Major Hugo Thurston's current agenda. As an elite commando with the Australian Armed Forces, Hugo was trained to make fast decisions and he made one now. As reading choice for his dinner companion, the book on granite seemed perfect.

Seemed. Make sure. His training said check the whole scene.

The reader wasn't alone. She was one of a pair, and both women looked less than thirty. This could mean trouble, especially when Maudie was with him.

But, on closer inspection, things looked even more promising. The book held by the second woman was *Prehistory in Stone.*

'We're sitting here,' he told the waiter, and before Maudie could object, her grandson shepherded her into the seats opposite the two readers. Hopefully they'd keep their noses in their books for the entire meal.

But even if they did, Hugo still didn't want to be here. He and his grandmother were travelling Platinum Class on the *Ghan*, the legendary train running through Australia's vast outback. Platinum service included gourmet meals served in their private sitting room.

But… 'Why would I want to eat my meals just with you?' Maudie had demanded.

'We have massive windows. You can look at the whole Australian outback while we eat.'

'The dining car has windows, too, and I like meeting people. If your grandfather was here, he'd have taken me to the dining car.' Maudie had groped for her handkerchief, and so, of course, the thing was decided. To the dining car they went, where tables were filled to capacity—which meant, Platinum Class or not, they had to share.

With Granite and Prehistory.

At least let this meal be better than lunch, he demanded silently of fate. It could hardly be worse. For their first meal on board they'd been stuck with a middle-aged couple who recognised Maud and exuded sympathy as a form of pleasantry.

'We read about your husband's death. Oh, you poor thing. But he had such a fabulous life. You can't really mourn someone so rich who dies so old, can you?'

Then, as Maudie failed to respond, they'd turned to Hugo. 'And you're home to take over your grandfather's company. It's about time. The gossip magazines have been wondering about you for years. No one's ever been able to understand why you've stayed in the army so long, and in such awful places. And what a waste when you're so rich...'

He'd wanted to do violence, but his grandmother's dignity had made him reply in an almost civilised fashion. Maudie had grown quiet with distress but she was one brave lady. She'd returned for dinner, to take another chance.

With Granite and Prehistory.

'Would it be an imposition if we sat with you?' Maudie asked the stone women, deferential, even though in the democracy of the train dining room there was no choice.

Granite gazed up from her book. She was in her late twenties, Hugo thought. Her fair hair was hauled into a scrappy bunch of curls which spoke of little effort, and the smile she offered was perfunctory. She looked…absent, he thought, and he wondered if she'd been ill.

'Hello,' she said softly. 'Of course you can sit here; isn't that right, Amy?'

The woman beside her—Amy?—lowered her book. They looked like sisters, Hugo thought. They were both slight, maybe five feet four or so. Both had soft blonde curls and clear brown eyes. They were both a little too thin.

What was more important than their appearance, though, was that neither looked gushers. Granite was already returning to her book.

The one called Amy, however, seemed slightly more interested. She glanced briefly at Hugo, and then at Maud.

Maud gazed back, eighty-three years old, recently bereaved and obviously anxious. Despite her assumed bravery, Sir James's death had devastated her, and the ordeal of lunch had left its mark.

Her eyes locked with Amy's.

Be nice to her, Hugo silently demanded, but he got no further. No silent demands were needed. Prehistory-transformed-into-Amy made her decision and she beamed a welcome.

And that beam…

She was exquisite, Hugo thought, as stunned as

if the sun had come out right over their table. She was simply, gloriously lovely.

Granite, the shadowed one, was wearing jeans, sneakers and a plain white shirt. Amy was dressed for comfort as well, but very differently, in black tights, ballet flats and a soft blue over-sized sweater. Her hair was looped into an unruly knot, with wispy curls tumbling free. Unlike her sister, she was wearing a little make-up. Her full lips were glossed the palest of pink and there was a touch of sparkle around her eyes.

But with a beam like hers, Hugo decided, Amy didn't need sparkle. Maudie was returning her smile, and what a smile.

Amy hadn't smiled at *him*, he thought.

Um…so what? He was here to keep Maudie happy, and if Amy could do it…

Please don't gush, he demanded silently of her. Please don't do the… *Oh, you're Dame Maud Thurston.*

She didn't.

'Save me from rocks,' she said simply.

Maudie smiled back. She slipped into the window seat and Hugo sat beside her, but no one was looking at him. Granite was back in her book and Amy had eyes only for Maudie.

'Rachel thinks I'll enjoy this journey more if I understand what I'm seeing,' she said, still beaming her pleasure at Maudie's arrival. 'But rocks…'

'We're seeing some interesting rocks,' Maudie ventured, and Hugo saw a hint of a twinkle in his grandmother's eyes.

A twinkle. That was what he was here for.

His grandmother had planned this journey with his grandfather, had looked forward to it, had persuaded her ailing husband it was just what he needed to restore his health, but tragically James had died four weeks before departure. Maudie had sunk into desolation so deep it scared him, and taking this journey in his grandfather's stead had seemed as good a way as any to distract her. So far it hadn't worked. Hugo hadn't seen Maudie smile for a month, yet here was her smile again, and he felt a knot unravel in his gut that he hadn't known had been knotted.

All his life he'd tried to stay detached, but right now he wasn't detached at all. In the face of his grandmother's grief he was helpless.

'You're a dancer,' she was saying to Amy in tones of discovery, and Amy's smile faded a little.

'Um…yes,' she admitted as Hugo looked on in

astonishment. Rather than the woman recognising Maudie, the situation was reversed.

'Oh, my dear, you're Amy Cotton.' Maudie seemed awed. 'You danced in *Giselle* last July. We went backstage and were introduced…'

'I was only in the corps de ballet,' Amy said, looking flabbergasted. 'How did you…'

'I know all our dancers,' Maudie said. 'And you've danced many more major roles. You used to be…'

'A long time ago I used to be,' Amy said flatly, her beam fading to nothing. 'And now I'm completely retired.'

'Oh, of course. Oh, my dear, I'm so sorry.' Maudie's twinkle gave way to distress. She reached across the table and touched Amy's hand, a fleeting touch of genuine contrition. 'You know my James died a month ago? Everyone keeps wanting to talk about his death and I hate it, yet here I am, the minute I see you, launching into talk of your retirement. At the level you danced, I know it must hurt almost as much as losing James. I'm so, so sorry. Can we talk about rocks again, or would you like to go back to your book?'

There was a moment's silence. Granite had looked up from her book and was watching Amy with concern. Not Granite. What had Amy called her? Rachel.

'You don't have to read it,' Rachel ventured. 'I only suggested it…'

'As a way to distract you?' Maudie ventured. 'Like my grandson keeps telling me to look out of the window. "Look, Gran, there's a camel," Hugo says, when all I'm seeing is James. But you know, even if it hurts to think of James—and it does—there's no way camels work as diversionary tactics. I suspect books on rocks might even be worse.'

Silence.

This could go either way, Hugo thought. They could all retreat and he could have the private lunch he craved, or…

Or maybe he was no longer fussed about a private lunch. Maybe these two had him intrigued.

Danger. One hint of interest, he told himself, and Maud would be away on her favourite pastime. Even his grandfather's death hadn't deflected her. These were two young women. *Young. Women.* Once upon a time Maudie had been fussy about who she threw at him. Now she was growing desperate. Young and women were the only two descriptors she needed, and the fact that Amy danced…

He needed, very carefully, to be uninterested. He needed to shut up and let Maudie do the talking—if Amy and Rachel would let her.

And it seemed they'd relented. Amy's smile returned, not on full beam, as it had been when welcoming an elderly lady to join her, but neutrally friendly now, treating his grandmother as an equal.

'I'm a bit touchy,' she admitted. 'And I'm sorry. I've been retired for three months now—you'd think I'd be over it. But your husband's death…' This time it was she who touched Maudie's hand. 'Sixty years of marriage to a man such as Sir James… You and your husband have done so much for our world. You can't imagine how grateful we've been, and you can't imagine how much he's missed.'

She smiled, then, a smile that was neither ingratiating nor patronising to the old. It was, Hugo thought, just right. 'I guess we all have to learn to cope with loss,' she said. She glanced fleetingly at her sister and an expression passed between them Hugo didn't have a hope of understanding. 'It never stops being gut-wrenching, but maybe we need to give the occasional rock and camel a chance.'

She glanced out of the window and suddenly her smile returned in full. 'And speaking of camels… Look!'

And out of the window four wild camels were loping along, keeping pace with the train.

Camels had been brought to Australia in the nineteenth century. Made unnecessary now by modern transport, they'd run wild and thrived in places where no other animal could survive.

'They're amazing,' Amy breathed as she watched the wild young camels race.

'Fantastic,' Maudie agreed, finally caught by the camels she'd scorned.

'They have camel races at Alice Springs,' Amy said regretfully. 'But there are no races while we're there. Rachel says we'll look at rocks instead.'

This was said with such a tone of martyrdom that Maudie laughed, and Rachel laughed—and even Hugo found himself smiling.

And then he thought: a ballet dancer who made them all smile. Uh oh.

Ballet was Maudie's passion. At six feet in her rather substantial bare feet, Maudie could never,

ever, have been a ballet dancer, but she adored it and she had a permanent booking for most major Australian performances.

As a kid, in the many times his father had offloaded him onto Maudie, she'd often taken Hugo with her.

He glanced across at Amy now and he thought: had this woman been one of those sylphlike figures whose movements on the stage were pure grace and beauty?

The last ballet he'd been to was when he'd been about sixteen. He'd been traumatised by the latest of his father's public scandals. His grandparents were the centre of media attention and, in typical teenage fashion, he'd decided every eye in the theatre was on him. He'd watched, sullen and uncooperative, but, despite himself, he'd found himself caught. He'd thought then, fleetingly, he knew why his grandmother loved it.

But, after that, he'd never been back. Real men didn't go to the ballet, especially men headed for the army, for the powerful SWAT team, for action in Iraq, Afghanistan, so many of the world's trouble spots.

Now, at thirty-seven, he was seeing a faint echo of a world he'd last seen twenty years ago.

Amy was talking to his grandmother as if she was already a friend. She'd figured just the right note. They shared sadness, yet both were moving on.

The sister—Rachel?—seemed a shadow on the periphery, polite but looking as if she'd love to retreat to her stones.

The impression of illness intensified.

He'd like to know these women's stories.

No. No, he wouldn't. He wanted to get this journey over with, get his grandmother cheered up and get back to his unit. His grandmother was doing everything she could to draw him into her world, and he would not be drawn.

Except the appalling woman they'd met at lunch had been right. Maybe he had no choice.

The camels won. They upped the pace, swept forward until they were a carriage ahead and then veered away, triumphant.

'I'm guessing they race every train,' Amy said, and she suddenly sounded wistful. 'Don't they look wonderful? Don't they look free?'

'They're young,' Maudie said, and the wistfulness was in her voice as well. 'They'll get aching legs soon enough.'

'Yep, any minute now they'll be taking anti-inflammatories and heating wheat bags to take to bed at night,' Amy said, and Maudie chuckled— and Hugo glanced at Amy and thought: there's pain behind those words. Pain and courage.

He did not want to be interested in a woman on a train.

Rachel was back in her book.

Amy was slipping steak into her purse.

Amy was *what?*

He must have imagined it.

He hadn't imagined it. She'd sliced a sliver, then dropped her hand below the table to where her purse lay on her knee. When she'd raised her fork the steak was gone.

She cut another sliver and ate it, just like normal.

The waiter appeared to take Maudie and Hugo's order. They were a course behind the girls. They could watch.

Rachel read. Amy and Maudie chatted.

A steak sliver raised to Amy's lips. Another.

Another went below the table and disappeared.

Hugo was trained to notice small details. Suspicions. Anything out of the ordinary could mean trouble. As tiny a detail as a robe worn slightly askew, or a guy smiling more widely than appropriate meant immediate caution.

He wasn't in a war zone now. He could hardly drag Amy's hand up with the offending steak and say, *Explain yourself.*

Another sliver dropped purse-wards. She glanced up and met his gaze. Their eyes locked.

She knew he'd seen.

She didn't say a word but there was a message in those clear brown eyes...

Please don't say anything. This is important. Please...

Curiouser and curiouser. A steak-smuggling, rock-reading ballet dancer.

Okay, he wasn't interested in women, at least not when he was around Maudie, but this was a mystery and maybe he could enjoy challenge without involvement.

His steak came. His grandmother had ordered fish. In the corner, Rachel had sent her quiche back uneaten.

On impulse, he cut a couple of slivers from the corner of his steak, dropped them into his napkin—then passed it under the table to Amy.

His fingers touched her knee. She met his gaze,

startled. His gaze locked, held; a silent message passed between them.

She dropped her hand under the table and found his.

The napkin passed between them and her eyes widened.

'Is anything wrong?' Maudie demanded, her sharp eyes missing little but not seeing the exchange. Only Amy's stillness.

'I... no,' Amy managed. 'Do you like your fish?'

'It's excellent,' Maudie said. 'Though the servings are too big. They always are.'

'But you finished all your steak, Miss Cotton,' Hugo said gravely.

'Amy,' she said, sounding distracted.

'Amy,' he said, liking the sound of it. 'I'm finishing mine, too. It's a long time till breakfast. They should provide midnight snacks. Maybe a steak sandwich in the small hours? I wonder if they have spare bread?'

She glared at him. His lips twitched. He had a mystery here and, despite his vow to stay uninvolved he sat back and started to enjoy himself.

'I've lost my napkin,' he told the waiter as he went past. 'Could I have another, please?'

Amy's glare intensified.

'So are you two getting off at Alice Springs?' Maudie was asking. This train went all the way north to Darwin, but many passengers broke the journey halfway to see the fabulous rock formations: Uluru, formerly known as Ayers Rock, The Olgas, Mount Connor...

'We are,' Amy said. 'Of course we are. We'll spend a few days exploring. So many big rocks... What could make Rachel happier?'

Rachel gave a fleeting smile, but it didn't reach her eyes.

'Will you climb Uluru?' Maudie asked her, but it was Amy who answered.

'Uluru's sacred to the indigenous people. They don't like anyone climbing. I'd love to climb the Olgas, though. Did you know European explorers named the Olgas after Queen Olga of Wurtenburg, when the local people named it Kata Tjuta thousands of years ago? Then they changed Uluru to Alice Springs, naming it after someone who never even came here. How weird is that?'

'Weird,' Hugo agreed, finding himself increasingly drawn into the conversation. This woman was passionate, he thought. There was enough indignation in those few words to show she cared.

And then he looked closer. In Afghanistan he'd trained himself to notice tribal differences. These two women had cute blonde curls, but their skin was darker than the complexion from Irish or English heritage. It wasn't the dark of fake tan; it was more a beautiful bronze brush. And Amy's nose, cute and snub, was a tiny bit flattened at the end. Another of those subtle hints.

'You have native blood,' he said, and suddenly, wow, here was her beam again. He loved this beam. How could he make it stay on?

'Well done, you,' Amy said. 'We're three-quarters Irish, but our maternal grandmother was from a tribe near Alice. She was taken away as a child, but she talked about Kata Tjuta and Uluru all our childhood.'

'She never came back?'

'Sadly, no. She died when we were still kids, but we always told her we'd come. And now, with Rachel's rocks…'

'You'll climb?'

'Kata Tjuta? Rachel might not be able to,' Amy said. 'She's been ill. But I will. Rachel wants rock samples, and I'll take photos.'

'Which is a problem all on its own,' Rachel volunteered from her shadows. 'Amy's photos tend to be smudgy pictures of clouds or of her trainers.'

'Oi. I'm better than that,' Amy retorted.

'Not much,' Rachel said darkly.

'My grandson takes wonderful photos,' Maudie said, and Hugo realised that, for the first time in the entire trip, Maudie sounded happy. And… thoughtful? Uh oh. He knew that tone. Maudie's Machiavellian matchmaking was about to go into overdrive. 'And I expect you need rock samples, Rachel, my dear.'

'I do,' Rachel said, and she smiled, too. It was a faint echo of her sister's smile, but she was no longer looking at her book. 'Uluru and Kata Tjuta are made of a type of sandstone known as arkose, with shiny crystals of pink feldspar mixed in. There's controversy about ageing. I have permission to take tiny traces to confirm composition.'

'Hugo could cart you down boulders,' Maudie said, in her element now and loving it. 'He's very strong. He's a commando, you know.'

'I thought commandos carted machine guns,' Rachel said, mystified.

'I cart steak,' Hugo said promptly. 'That's been my latest mission. Steak-smuggling.'

Amy choked, and then managed to swallow

laughter enough to glare at her sister. 'We're not here to age rocks,' she retorted. 'We're here on holiday.'

'So are we, dear,' Maudie said serenely. 'Are you staying at the Uluru resort?'

'We have a room in the budget hostel...'

'Oh, no, dear, that'll never do,' Maudie broke in, and Hugo thought: uh oh. Uh oh, uh oh, uh oh. But there was no way of stopping Maudie once she was on a mission. 'Hugo and I are staying at Thurston House, a homestead set up for senior management when they need a base out here. It's a lovely self-contained house complete with pool, staff and staff quarters. But Hugo may need to visit one of our mines and I hate being there alone. But you, dear...' She fixed her suddenly gimlet eyes on Rachel. 'Do you play Scrabble?'

'I...yes,' Rachel admitted, sounding confused. 'But...'

'No,' Amy said firmly. 'We don't.'

'We do,' Rachel said, even more confused.

'Well, yes,' Amy said, exasperated. 'Rachel loves words almost as much as she loves rocks. When I walk out of a room, I leave, but Rachel absquatulates. And if you think I'm making that up, she added ab and ulate to my pathetic squat and achieved untold fame in the Great Cotton Scrabble Challenge of 2007. But if you're offering us alternative accommodation, thank you very much but Rachel and I are self-sufficient.'

'But if your sister's been ill, she'll feel bad that she can't go off and do things with you,' Maudie countered. This was like watching a train wreck, Hugo thought. It was about to happen, whether he jumped onto the tracks or not. 'Like I feel bad when I can't accompany Hugo. You'll be doing us a huge favour if you stay with us. There are four bedrooms and they're massive. Hugo's organised a car to meet the train. We could travel down there together, the four of us, and have fun.'

'Maud!' Train wreck or not, he did step into the line of impending disaster then. 'We can't…'

'Neither can we,' Amy said faintly. 'Thank you but…'

'But we have twenty-four hours to change your mind,' Maudie said happily. 'You don't want to stay in a backpackers', do you, Rachel?'

'No, but…'

'There you are, then. Meanwhile, if you feel like Scrabble in the morning, we're in Platinum Cabins Car Two, Cabins Four and Five, with a nice little sitting room in the middle. There's a butler person who guards our privacy but just ask for us and Hugo will okay it. He'll more than okay it. It'll be lovely.'

Maudie beamed and her beam almost matched Amy's, only Amy's wasn't on. Amy was now looking trapped—which was pretty much how Hugo was feeling.

'I need to go to bed,' Rachel said, still sounding confused. 'If you'll excuse me...'

'If you'll excuse us both,' Amy said with alacrity and stood. 'Thank you for the lovely offer, Dame Maud, but, of course, we can't accept. Our accommodation's already paid for, and we're content. Goodnight.'

She backed to leave the table, but there was something Hugo needed to say. He'd been slicing for a while now. 'Amy?'

Amy paused. 'Yes?'

He shouldn't say anything. He should simply let things finish right now, but this was irresistible.

'Here's a little something for midnight,' he said, and he handed over his second carefully wrapped napkin.

Amy stared down at it. If it was possible for her to look any more hunted, she did.

'Thank you,' she said and stuffed it into her purse.

She turned and fled, with Rachel following limply behind.

'What nice girls,' Maudie said as they retreated.

'Yes.' But needy. He'd kind of like more steak.

'It'll be nice to have company at Uluru.'

'They refused.' Praise be.

'They don't mean it. Amy's worried about Rachel. You can see it. She'll like Rachel having a nice quiet time with me while you take her off exploring. You'll have time. I know you're thinking of visiting the mine, but there'll be days to spare. I wonder what's wrong with Rachel?'

'It's none of our business.'

'Of course it's our business. Amy's part of the ballet company your grandfather and I practically founded. I usually keep track of the members of our company and it was a shock to hear she's retired. Since James fell ill, of course, I haven't heard a thing. I need to get back in touch. But then, it's her sister who looks ill. She's not in the ballet scene. If I wasn't on this train I could make some phone calls...'

'It's not our business!' he repeated.

'Of course it is,' she snapped. 'They're two nice

girls and anyone can see they're in trouble. It's our job to help them. And it was very nice of you to give Amy your steak.'

'I…' She'd seen, then. He might have known.

No. Not worth arguing.

'Though cold steak will be horrid as a late night snack,' Maudie said, and he could tell she'd already included the girls in her list of responsibilities. Maudie's principal skill was picking people up and making them feel better. Hugo loved her for it, but every now and then it got her into trouble. And now, like always…

Now he hadn't a snowball's chance in a bushfire of stopping her.

'If Amy wants to bully Rachel into eating later on, she'd be better with sweets,' she was saying thoughtfully. 'We have complimentary chocolates in our sitting room. Do you think you should take them some?'

'No. I don't know where to find them.'

'You can find them if you want to.'

'I don't want to.'

'Hugo…' Her voice was filled with reproach.

'No.'

'What a waste,' she said sadly. But her indomitable spirit had been stirred and it wasn't about to settle. 'Still,' she said thoughtfully. 'We'll probably see them at breakfast and if we don't then I'll track them down. And the house at Uluru... The more I think of it, the more perfect it seems.' She smiled again, the smile that Hugo had wanted to return, but the smile that now meant trouble. 'We might just have some fun, and heaven knows we all need it.'

Fun, Hugo thought.

He'd wanted his grandmother to have fun, but now he wasn't too sure what fun entailed. Trouble?

Two single women and Maudie? Trouble indeed.

CHAPTER TWO

'SO TELL me who they are,' Rachel demanded.

To say Amy was disconcerted was an understatement. She needed to catch her breath, get her composure back and feed Buster.

Instead, for the first time in this trip, for the first time in months, she had her sister asking questions.

But Buster first. She locked their compartment door, opened the wardrobe and Buster nosed out.

Buster was a tiny fox terrier, the size of half a cat. He was fourteen years old, he was missing an ear and he had one gammy leg.

Rachel had found him over twelve years ago. He'd been tossed from a car like litter, and Rachel had come home holding the bedraggled creature as if he were diamonds.

'Amy, we have to keep him. We have to. Please let me...'

They'd been staying with the last of their succession of foster parents and, as usual, Amy had pleaded on behalf of her younger sister.

'He'll stay outside. I can build him a kennel. We can use my allowance to feed him. I swear he'll be no trouble.'

The couple they'd been staying with had been one of their kinder sets of foster parents and he'd been allowed to stay. At night they'd sneaked him in through their bedroom window. He'd slept with them then, and he'd been with them since.

Rachel had left him behind two years ago—he'd stayed with Amy during her sister's doomed marriage—but they were together again now, and it was Rachel who needed Buster rather than the other way round.

The little dog nosed out of the tiny wardrobe and looked around with caution, as if he understood he was in hiding. Then his ears pricked and his disreputable tail started to wag.

He'd been on dog pellets for two days. He was clever. The smell from Amy's purse was not dog pellets.

'It's rump steak,' she said, and grinned. 'With a tiny smear of béarnaise sauce for m'lor's satisfaction.' She set it on the table napkin on the floor.

Buster looked up at them first, his great brown eyes adorably expressive. His wagging tail meant he wagged his whole body. Joy was Buster and rump steak, and even Rachel was smiling.

But... 'So who are they?' she asked again and Amy thought: nope, she wasn't about to be deflected.

'The old lady's Dame Maud Thurston,' she told her sister. 'She's been a major patron of the Australian ballet for as long as I can remember. She's a gem, and her husband was just as lovely. He made a fortune from mining—you must know Thurston Holdings—and together they've run one of the biggest charitable foundations in Australia. It's not just the ballet that benefits.'

'And the guy?'

For some reason Amy wasn't sure of talking about the guy. He'd made her...edgy. 'That'd be her grandson,' she said.

'So tell me about him.' Rachel perched on her seat and hugged her knees.

Rachel? Interested in a guy?

A waft of remembrance flooded back, making Amy wince. Two years ago, Rachel had come backstage after a performance, her normal prosaic, academic self starry-eyed about the Spanish dancer who'd danced opposite Amy. 'Tell me about him. Can you introduce me?'

It was the beginning of a tragedy which had left Rachel with shattered dreams and aching loss. Now… She must have seen what Amy was thinking because she rushed in.

'I don't mean that,' she said, sounding angry. 'He's gorgeous but you needn't think I'm ever going down that path again. And it's you he's interested in.'

'He isn't.'

'He is.'

'Rachel…'

'Okay, he isn't,' Rachel said, and astonishingly she was smiling. 'But you know about him. Tell me all.'

'We're not staying with them at Uluru.'

'Of course we're not,' Rachel said equably. 'But tell me about him all the same.'

'I don't know much. Only what's spread in ballet circles and that's only as much as affects the ballet. We're a self-centred lot.'

'But you do know something.'

She nodded, strangely reluctant. What was it about the guy that made her want to shut up, not probe further? But Rachel was interested and, the way Rachel had been for the last twelve months, any interest at all was to be encouraged.

'The family's been in the media for ever,' she said, thinking it through as she spoke. 'I don't read gossip mags but because they're important to the ballet world, I can't help but keep up with them. Sir James owns…owned… Thurston Holdings. You know it's one of the biggest mining corporations in the world? It's also the most principled. Thurston's has a reputation for fair dealings, for treating their people right, for restoring land after mining's finished. Sir James and Dame Maud have tried to keep a low profile but, with that much money, that much power, it's impossible.'

'I have heard of them,' Rachel admitted, which was a huge concession from someone who spent her life in books. 'I did hear Sir James had died—it was all over the papers. So Hugo's the grandson. Is his dad taking over the reins?'

'That's just it,' Amy told her. 'He's dead. Bertram was a disaster but we know nothing about this guy.'

'We?'

Amy flushed. She was no longer part of the Australian ballet scene, she told herself. Move on.

But Rachel wanted to know, and this wasn't ballet. She could force herself to gossip a little.

'The Thurston Corporation sponsors so much—

the ballet, the theatre, sports for the disabled, medical research… So many organisations rely on them. But when Bertram was alive and we thought he'd inherit, it seemed like it'd all stop as soon as Sir James died.'

'So Bertram was Hugo's dad?'

'Yep.' Amy settled back onto her seat-cum-bed and decided she might as well recall all she knew. 'According to gossip, Bertram was wild. Really wild. He was into parties, gambling, drugs, all the things his parents weren't. His marriage lasted about two minutes—rumour is his wife suicided later on, but it could have been an overdose. She was a media bimbo. That set a pattern for Bertram. He moved from woman to woman, every one of them media darlings, every one of them self-destructing on the lifestyle. It must have broken his parents' hearts, but there was no way they could stop him. He finally did the same.'

'Why did I not know this?' Rachel demanded.

'Because most of it happened when we were kids,' Amy said patiently. 'I only know because Bertram died in unsavoury circumstances about eight years ago. By then he was so burnt out that even the gossip mags weren't interested, except to up their interest in Hugo. But I was a baby dancer then, and I heard the relief in dance circles. Our director was trying hard not to be ecstatic. His take was that we'd have more chance of continued support from an unknown grandson than we ever had from Bertram. But Hugo didn't come home, even then. He's been in the army since he was a teenager, in some secret unit no one knows about. He's made a couple of flying visits since and the press has gone nuts every time—Australia's most eligible bachelor, that sort of thing—but he's always looked like he hates it. There was a fuss when he came home for his grandfather's funeral, but then he went to ground again. Everyone's wondered what will happen to Thurston Holdings—and lo, here he is, on our train.'

'Home to pick up where his grandfather left off?' Rachel said doubtfully. 'He doesn't look like a businessman about to sponsor the ballet. He looks…tough.'

'Like a warrior,' Amy agreed, starting to enjoy herself. They were safely back in their cabin. Why not let herself wallow? 'I was thinking that,' she confessed, letting her mind meander over the man she'd just met. 'That gorgeous, deep black hair, sun-bleached at the tips. All those muscles… And he's weathered and so fit it's scary. The bone structure of his face—it's like it's sculpted. It must be from years of living hard. And did you see the way his shirt strained? No shirt's ever been built to accommodate that type of chest.' She grinned at Rachel, enjoying startling her. 'And those blue eyes with crinkles at the edges like he spends his time looking into the sun… Whew.'

'You really did look at him,' Rachel breathed, stunned.

'Um…yep. There's no harm in admiring beauty,' she admitted. 'A girl can admire—from a distance.'

Rachel's smile widened. Maybe she was starting to enjoy herself as well.

'I guess he'll have spent his life looking into the sun through machine gun sights,' she suggested. 'That'd make anyone's eyes crinkle.'

'I bet you're right,' Amy agreed. 'And field glasses. He'll have stood in dugouts in the searing sun, field glasses trained for the enemy…'

'Or on hilltops?'

'I don't think you look for the enemy on hilltops,' Amy said doubtfully. 'Wouldn't you get shot? It'd be such a shame to shoot a body like that.'

'It would,' Rachel said definitely. 'No one could

shoot such a man. Did you see the muscles on his arms?' Rachel was following on with relish. 'Maybe that's from hand-to-hand combat?'

'With sumo wrestlers,' Amy guessed. 'I'd imagine he takes on ten every morning before breakfast.'

'And now we've taken his steak,' Rachel said mournfully. 'Buster, how could you?' She giggled and Amy thought wow, her sister was giggling. She giggled back and it was a gorgeous moment.

And then a camel hove into view. Another one, racing the train.

But only one?

In the dining car they'd been able to see out both sides of the train. Now, back in their tiny compartment, they could only see the right side of the train.

Rachel was looking out, entranced, at the lone camel and Amy couldn't resist; she opened the door to the corridor to see if more camels were racing on the far side.

There were. Five of them.

'Oh,' Rachel breathed. 'I wonder if Maudie's seeing...'

'Buster!'

And for one fatal moment they'd been distracted. For one moment they'd had the door wide open and had been staring in delight at camels.

And Buster, fourteen years old, sleeping out his days content to be with the people he loved and the occasional sunbeam, had just had rump steak for dinner—and he'd looked up and seen camels!

The camels were gaining on the train. They were stretching out away from the near windows.

And Buster, a tiny dog in spirit but a guard dog at heart, went flying along the corridor in pursuit, barking as if he were a hound in full cry.

No!

Amy flew along the corridor after him, her heart in her mouth. Luckily, the end of the carriage was the door through to the next car. He could go no further—but he was still barking.

No!

She reached him and scooped him up and tucked him under her sweater, just as compartment doors started to open.

'A dog…' An elderly man with a walking stick was staring in horror in both directions. 'Did you see a dog? Who's barking?'

'It must have been outside the train,' Amy said, beetling past him with her bulge held away. Praying his eyesight wasn't good.

'I heard a dog.' It was a young mother. 'I hate dogs. Our Polly's allergic.'

'I didn't see a dog,' Amy lied and bolted for their compartment.

'Did you see a dog?' the young woman demanded of Rachel, who was outside their compartment looking worried.

'It was racing the camels,' Rachel managed, trying to retreat as well. 'I think it was a dingo.'

'But it sounded like it was in the train,' the woman said. 'I think you should report it to the conductor.'

'I need to go to bed,' Rachel said, and retreated into the compartment after Amy.

She slammed the door, still giggling.

But Amy wasn't giggling. That had been too close for comfort.

She knew it had been a really bad plan to bring Buster, but what choice did she have? Rachel had hugged Buster since she'd come home from hospital. Rachel's life was hugging her dog and reading her textbooks.

The *Ghan* had been a dream they'd shared since they were children, to travel through the outback, to see their grandmother's birthplace, to see the rocks Rachel loved.

It might just haul her out of her misery, Amy had thought, and it was starting to, but ooh, Buster-smuggling could cause complications. Rachel was giggling, but at what price?

'She won't go find the conductor,' Rachel decreed. 'She won't leave those appalling children. I've met them in the bathroom and they're awful.'

'The other guy might.'

'It doesn't matter. Buster's hidden now. He's safe.' Rachel looked fondly at Buster, who was peering innocently out from under Amy's sweater. 'What a good thing you wore that.'

'It has its uses. But if anyone searches…'

'They won't. And they don't need to come in here. It's not like we're in a classy cabin that has turn downs.'

They weren't. They'd requested their beds stay up all the time—'as Rachel needs to rest'. No one needed to come near them.

And Rachel was smiling.

Okay, she could live with this.

'Bed,' Rachel said. 'Buster can come under the covers with me. If anyone looks in, we're fast asleep.'

'I'd like a shower,' Amy said doubtfully. 'But I might wait for a few minutes, just to be sure.'

'You do that,' Rachel said and retired to her bunk, Buster with her.

Amy waited for half an hour, holding her breath the whole time.

Nothing.

Rachel and Buster fell asleep.

Okay, they were fine.

She took her towel and pyjamas to the bathroom at the end of the carriage. She showered and washed her hair. She also tried, weirdly, not to think about Hugo. Which was nuts. She had enough to think about without worrying about Hugo Thurston.

She'd seen Rachel smile. She should be happy.

She *was* happy. She emerged from the bathroom feeling clean and determinedly cheerful.

The conductor was emerging from the second compartment.

'Miss,' he said as he saw her, 'have you seen a dog?'

Miss stopped in her tracks. To say she felt at a disadvantage was an understatement. She was wearing pink satin pyjamas with cream lace trimming, with fluffy pink flip-flops to match. She'd bought Rachel beautiful nightwear when she'd moved from hospital to rehab. Normally Amy slept in a T-shirt and knickers, but on the train, with a shared bathroom, Rachel had decreed they'd share her pretty ones.

So she was respectable—almost—but she didn't feel respectable. She felt numb with panic. She stared down at her pink-painted toenails in her fluffy pink flip flops and tried to decide what to say.

Had she seen a dog?

'Um…no,' she lied.

'We've had a report there's a dog in this carriage,' the man said. 'I've had orders to search.'

'Ooh,' Amy managed. 'Have you searched us?'

'You're in?'

'Compartment Seven.'

'I've done One and Two,' the guy said grimly. 'I'll get to you in a minute.'

'There's no need. My sister's asleep. She's been ill. Please don't disturb her.'

'Orders are to search the whole carriage.'

'But…'

'No exceptions.'

'Okay,' Amy said faintly. 'Just search quietly in Seven. Oh, and I might not be there. I have… I have a date.'

* * *

It was ten o'clock and Hugo was going stir crazy.

Maudie was exhausted. She'd headed straight to bed after dinner, to her lovely little bedroom just through the sitting room door. Hugo had a similar bedroom. They had their own palatial bathroom. Luxury.

But Hugo didn't do luxury. He was accustomed to swags on the ground, to sleeping rough. He'd had over a month of soft living since his grandfather's death had brought him home, and he wasn't enjoying it any better now than he had at the start.

He was also bored out of his mind, aching to be back with his unit.

He had a television. Who wanted to sit on the *Ghan* and watch telly?

He had a murder mystery to read but he'd already figured out the murderer. What fun was there in that?

He could go to the lounge car and meet people. Yeah, right.

Scrabble was the last of an appalling list of alternatives but he found himself organising letters. Trying to remember how to spell absquatulate.

Thinking of a brown-eyed dancer with an appetite for cold steak.

He found himself grinning, and he hauled himself back from the brink with a jerk. If Maudie even suspected what he was thinking...

He was not thinking.

A knock on the door. Yes! Anything to escape this boredom. He flung the door wide, so hard the man behind stepped back in alarm.

It was Henry, the Platinum butler. I bet his name's not really Henry, Hugo thought. I bet all Platinum butlers are Henry.

The guy was struggling. He wanted to say something but was having trouble getting it out.

'Yes,' Hugo said encouragingly.

'Sir...'

'Can I help you?'

'There's a woman,' Henry said, sounding torn. 'In pyjamas. She says you've invited her to your room.'

There was a moment's stillness while they both took that in.

'A woman,' Hugo said at last. 'In pyjamas.'

'A young woman.' He might sound the same if he was announcing the arrival of aliens.

'Did she give a name?' Hugo asked cautiously.

The man's face cleared. 'Yes,' he said. 'Yes, she did. She says her name is Amy Cotton and she's a friend of Dame Maud. She says you're expecting her. She's carrying a large purse and she says she has something Dame Maud needs.'

'And she's wearing pyjamas.'

'Yes, sir,' the guy said. 'Pink ones.' He groped for his dignity and managed to look disapproving. 'My job's to protect your privacy, sir. Shall I tell her to go away?'

It's Amy, Hugo thought. It's a brown-eyed girl who made his grandmother's eyes twinkle. It's Amy, in pink pyjamas, carrying a purse.

Should he tell her to go away?

He definitely ought to. But…

'I expect she's bringing my grandmother notes on cooking steak sandwiches,' he said at last. 'Maybe even ingredients. We were…discussing it at dinner. Where is she now?'

'At the end of the carriage. No one's allowed past the butler's pantry without authorisation.'

'Then she has my authorisation,' Hugo said. 'Go on, man, let her through.'

What did the guy think she was? A call girl operating on the train? A woman carrying her credit card facilities in her oversized purse as she wandered from carriage to carriage in her satin pyjamas?

Crazy or not, she had no choice but to be here.

By the time she'd got back to the compartment she and Rachel shared, the conductor had reached Compartment Four. She'd grabbed Buster, shoved him into her huge purse, waited for the conductor to come out of Compartment Four and go into Five, and then fled.

Successfully? Only if Hugo let her in. Only if he helped.

But the conductor had seen her go. She'd just reached the end of the carriage when she'd heard him call, 'Miss…'

She hadn't stopped.

The Thurstons were in Car Two. She and Rachel were in Car Six. She'd practically run the length of the train. And now here she was, stuck in the butler's pantry, waiting for Hugo to say yes he'd receive visitors. If not, she was facing disaster.

What would they do if they found Buster? Put him off the train? Put her and Rachel off as well?

What was the penalty for dog-smuggling?

The authorities could hardly toss them to the camels, she thought, but there'd be bleak little settlements in the middle of nowhere where they could be put out. There'd be a long wait for the next train, dubious accommodation and an expensive cartage fee to get Buster home.

Then what?

They needed to get to Darwin. She didn't have the money to pay for flights.

She was stuck in the Platinum butler's pantry waiting for the Thurston billions to decide her fate.

Maud would help her, she thought, but Maud might be asleep by now.

And Hugo? The warrior? Would he help—or not?

The longer the wait, the worse she felt. This was ghastly. She wanted clothes. She wanted out of here. Of all the stupid…

'Miss Cotton?'

She looked up and blessedly, magically, Hugo was striding along the corridor towards her. The butler was bustling behind him.

'M…Mr Thurston?' Her voice was practically a squeak.

'I believe you have a delivery for me.'

'I…' She gazed down at her purse and prayed Buster wouldn't wriggle. 'Yes.' If he demanded she hand it over here she was in real trouble.

'Excellent,' he said gravely. 'Would you like to

bring it to our sitting room yourself? I'm sure my grandmother will want to thank you. If you'll excuse us, Henry, I can take care of Miss Cotton from here.'

She was in a billionaire warrior's domain. She was wearing pink pyjamas and fluffy flip-flops, and she was carrying a dog in her purse.

Hugo was looking at her as if she were an unexploded bomb. As well he might.

He'd closed the door behind them. Somewhat wildly, she looked about her.

She'd read about these suites when she'd booked. The compartment was gorgeous—railway opulence at its most fabulous. If she'd had the money she could have booked a beautiful sitting room that turned into a bedroom at night, and if she'd had even more money she could have hired separate bedrooms so the sitting room stayed as it was.

This guy would have even more money. This man was a Thurston. He wouldn't get kicked off the train and have to rely on camels for transport.

'I'm thinking you brought me back my steak,' Hugo said, gently now. He was watching her bag with fascination. Buster had just wriggled.

'Sort of,' she managed. 'I mean…well…your

steak is definitely inside there. In a fashion. Look, I'm really sorry, but I'm desperate.'

'Really?' A twinkle was lurking deep in those weather-creased blue eyes. Man amused by idiot.

But then… 'How can I help?' he asked, and she almost fell on his neck. Of all the words she most wanted to hear, these were the sweetest.

'Hide my dog?'

'Your dog.' His lips twitched again. He had the most expressive mouth, she thought. At dinner he'd spent most of his time trying not to look grim. Now… She might be the village idiot but he found her amusing and if she could use that…

'We smuggled our dog on board,' she said.

'You know, I was starting to figure that, though I wasn't actually sure of the species. Cat? I wondered. Or python? Maybe taking your python back to his ancestral home.'

'Just a dog.' There didn't seem anything else to say.

'A purse-sized dog.'

'I can hardly fit a St Bernard in here,' she snapped and then bit her lip. 'Sorry. I'm stressed.'

'I can see that you are,' he said, even more gently. 'Can I see your dog?'

She looked into his face and saw laughter—

and knew suddenly that there was no way she'd be thrown to the camels when this guy was around. She took a deep breath and opened her purse.

Buster's nose appeared, then his whole head. He bobbed up and gazed around with interest, noted the proximity of the plush armchair and dived neatly downward. He sat, the picture of innocence, inspecting the Scrabble board as if he could read the letters.

'He...he looks a well-trained dog,' Hugo said faintly.

'I...yes.'

'Can he spell absquatulate?'

The tension faded a little. Not too much, though. This man was big. Seriously big.

In the dining car he'd worn a jacket and tie, in deference to his grandmother, she guessed, but here... His silver-grey silk tie had been tugged loose and the top buttons of his shirt were undone. His chest was as brown and sun-weathered as his face, and his muscles were clearly delineated under the soft cotton of his shirt.

He filled this tiny sitting room. And he was so close...

She was accustomed to lean, fit men—she lived in a world of dancing, where strength and fitness were everything—but in this man there was an extra dimension.

Sheer, tough grit.

She'd joked about it with Rachel. Suddenly the jokes faded.

She was in a tiny sitting room, in her pyjamas, with a man who looked what he was. A warrior.

Where was she? she thought wildly. What had he asked? Buster. Spelling. Absquatulate. She was out of control anyway, and the dumb question made her feel dizzy.

'He could if he wanted to,' she managed. 'But he may not bother. He has a well-honed instinct for what's important.'

'Like keeping away from butlers.'

'Yeah,' she managed. 'But not for keeping his head below the parapet. I... he decided to chase a camel.'

'A camel...'

'He didn't understand,' she said, aware she was sounding hysterical but there wasn't a thing she could do about it. 'The camels were outside the train and he was in. We opened the door out into the corridor to see them and he went haring out after them. And he barked.'

'As any well-trained dog would with a camel,'

Hugo said gravely, but his mouth twitched in a way she was starting to recognise. And like. Like a lot.

She was trying to explain. She had to focus really hard on what she was saying. This man was seriously disconcerting.

'I grabbed him and stuck him under my sweater,' she continued valiantly.

'I did wonder why you were wearing a sweater on a heated train.'

'My sweater's just for emergencies. He's great in my purse.'

'You're leaving him in your purse for the whole trip?'

'No,' she said, indignant. 'We leave him out in our little compartment. We have a pet mat for him to pee on and he's very good. I just take the pet mat to the bathroom when I need to.'

'Under your sweater?' He sounded fascinated. At least he hadn't thrown her out yet, she thought, feeling a tiny bit less desperate.

He was humouring the lunatic.

'He's neat,' she said, sounding defensive. 'It's easy.'

'Until it comes to camels.'

'Yes,' she admitted and met his gaze—and then

looked down at Buster. Because for some reason she couldn't hold that gaze.

What was it with this guy?

She'd danced with some of the best-looking males in the world. As a ballerina, she was accustomed to being skin-close. Here, she wasn't even skin-close to this man, but her body, for some weird reason, was starting what seemed a slow burn.

He had her totally disconcerted. He was still gazing at her dog. His dark hair was thick and wavy, and she had the most absurd desire to touch it, to run her fingers through and see how it felt.

Was she out of her mind? This guy was a billionaire. She was here in her pyjamas to ask for his help. A sexual come-on was maybe—just maybe—totally, absolutely, unquestionably out of the question.

'They're great pyjamas,' he said inconsequentially. 'Cute.'

'They're Rachel's.' What else was a girl to say?

'She has great taste. Tell me why you have a dog on the train.'

And he'd turned from fun to serious, just like that. The twinkle had faded and he wanted answers.

He deserved them.

He was looking at her again—*at her*—and his gaze was implacable. Not harsh, though, she thought, or even judgemental. She had a feeling she knew how this guy would operate in action; how he'd ask for answers from his men.

His underlings could come to this man if they were in trouble, she thought. But if they'd been stupid?

Stupid or not, she needed his help and he deserved the truth.

Why did she have a dog on this train? The answer was simple—and dreadful.

'My sister was in a car crash twelve months ago,' she told him baldly, not trying to conceal the emotion she still felt. 'Her husband was drink-driving and Rachel was seven months pregnant. She broke her pelvis and lost her baby. Her marriage ended. She's a trained geologist but her pregnancy and accident meant she lost her job. She's spiralled into depression and I was desperate to do something to distract her. We've decided to move to Darwin and somehow I managed to talk her into taking the trip on this train first. But Buster has been with us since childhood. We couldn't come without him.'

She glanced down at the little dog and her smile returned, just like that. Buster did that for her. 'Buster's our one true thing,' she said. 'He's old and placid and no trouble to anyone. So...'

'There are kennels and carrier companies to fly animals.'

'There are,' she agreed. 'But you try talking Rachel into using them. We've both ached to see Uluru. Rachel's research means she should see these places. This train's been a dream for a long, long time, but she won't leave Buster to do it.'

'So you gambled.'

'Yes,' she said and tilted her chin. 'And it's worth it. Rachel's smiled this trip, and her smile's reached her eyes for the first time since she lost the baby. Even if we get thrown off now, it's still been worth it.'

'I doubt they'll throw you off.'

'We're budget passengers. Of course they'll throw us off.'

He fell silent, watching her with those cool blue eyes. He was weighing her story, she thought. Weighing her?

'And you came to me why?' he asked at last.

'You and your grandmother are the only people I know on the train.'

'You don't know us.'

'Dame Maud knows me.'

'Maud's asleep.'

She stared down at her pink flip-flops and tried to make herself think. Tried to figure a way out of this mess that didn't involve this guy.

Tried to figure why she'd ever run to him in the first place.

A knock sounded on the door and she jumped.

'Yes?' Hugo sounded wary—as well he might.

'Mr Thurston, we need to speak to you.'

We. Uh oh. Amy's heart sank. It was the Platinum butler's voice but we meant a deputation. She must have been seen.

Criminal sighted fleeing carriage in pink pyjamas, carrying dog-sized purse.

When all else failed, face the music. She squared her shoulders and turned towards the door but, before she could take a step, Hugo had scooped Buster up and opened the inner door to the bedroom beyond. 'Don't move,' he hissed.

'Give us a moment, gentlemen,' he called, and disappeared. She heard an urgent murmur from within, and then he was back, without dog.

Don't move? She'd have to be stupid to move.

Whatever was happening, whatever he intended, she wasn't getting in his way.

She watched, stunned, as he upended her purse, brushing out stray dog hairs. He thrust a book inside and a couple of magazines as well, manoeuvring them so they made the purse bulge.

'Sit,' he told her, and she didn't have a choice, for he put his hands on her shoulders and forced her downward.

She sat.

For one millisecond he gazed down at her, his eyes a question. Then he seemed to answer himself. He undid a couple more buttons of his shirt. A wicked grin flickered beneath the set purpose of his gaze and, before she could stop him, he'd flicked open the top buttons of her pyjama top as well. He exposed cleavage. He exposed enough cleavage to make her almost indecent!

'Wh…'

'Hush,' he said, and then more firmly, 'hush, my lady of the night. You need to look…' He stood back and looked at her, considering. 'I know how you need to look.'

He stooped and placed his mouth on hers.

He kissed her.

CHAPTER THREE

To say she was shocked would be an understatement. To say she was thrown into a dimension she hadn't known existed would still be an understatement.

One minute Amy was figuring out how she could face a livid train conductor with her illegal dog. The next... Hugo Thurston's mouth was on hers.

There was no permission asked or granted. His hands were hard on her shoulders and he was kissing her whether she wanted to be kissed or not. His mouth was claiming hers. He was drawing her into him and he was possessing her with power and heat and sheer magnetic lust.

She was being kissed by Hugo Thurston?

How had this happened? She had no idea. She should struggle—but that'd mean somehow she had to figure out what was going on, and right now all she could think of was this kiss.

The heat. The power. The sheer magnetic pull.

She was melting into a man she'd met only hours ago. He was kissing her as if she was the most desirable woman...*and she was responding?*

Of course she was responding. How could she fail to respond? From the moment his mouth touched hers, from the moment his arms tugged her close, through shock she felt herself melt.

It was as if every nerve in her body was short circuiting. The heat from her lips was arcing out, up, down, around her body, causing every nerve-ending to cease functioning.

No. They were still functioning, she thought, dazed beyond belief. It was just that they were totally centred, totally focused, totally fused on this mouth that was claiming hers.

Such a kiss...

She'd been kissed before—of course she had—but never by a great weathered warrior of a man, a guy who oozed testosterone, whose strength was like an aura around him. A man whose eyes had gleamed once at her as he lowered his head, his gleam a dare, a challenge shooting from those blue, blue eyes.

She wasn't thinking straight. How could she think straight? His mouth was plundering hers.

His tongue was searching for entry and discovering a response in her that almost overwhelmed her.

She felt herself arch a little, her body automatically demanding to be nearer. Instinctively, involuntarily, her hands reached and found the thick thatch of his sun-bleached hair and she felt herself glorying in the silkiness, the strength. As if she was another woman, someone she didn't recognise, couldn't recognise, she felt herself deepen the kiss, and she felt a low burn start in her body. The flicker flared and built.

And then the contact broke, just like that.

He put her away from him, the gleam still in his eyes. He was laughing at her, she thought. Laughing!

His hand went to his belt buckle and twisted it undone—and then he turned to the door.

As he tugged it open he was fastening his belt again. He was glancing around at her, as if checking she was…respectable?

She wasn't respectable. He'd set the scene, she thought, stunned beyond belief. He'd made it look like…

She knew what it looked like. He was re-fastening his belt clumsily. She was sprawled, stunned, in the armchair, her pyjamas only just decent. She was flushed and dazed and her mouth felt bruised.

She felt—and she looked, she suspected—thoroughly, totally kissed.

She couldn't help it. She raised her hand to her lips and Hugo's smile deepened. He winked—the toe-rag winked!—before turning back to the men at the door.

It was Henry and the conductor from her carriage.

'Gentlemen,' he said, urbane and polite. But his annoyance was unmistakable for all that. 'How can I help?'

The scene was being played out to a nicety, Amy thought, unable to move. No one could doubt what had been happening in this room. No one could doubt why it had taken Hugo so long to answer the door.

'I'm so sorry…' Henry started, but the conductor behind him was made of sterner stuff. Maybe he wasn't quite as intimidated by the Thurston billions.

'The girl you're with,' he growled, and pointed to Amy. 'That woman. We have reason to believe she's carrying a dog.'

'A dog?' If they'd announced life on Mars, Hugo

could hardly have sounded more stunned. 'Amy has a dog?'

'Miss Cotton,' the conductor snapped. 'She's budget class.'

Hugo froze.

Once upon a time Amy had seen a frail, elderly Sir James Thurston escort his wife through a crowd of post-ballet revellers. A photographer had suddenly emerged from the throng and shoved his camera so close to Dame Maud that she'd spilled her drink.

Frail, elderly Sir James had suddenly been frail and elderly no longer. If there was ever any proof needed about the power needed to make the billions, it was there in that moment, when one blustering photographer was reduced to a whimpering puddle of humiliation.

And here it was again: the Thurston power. The stance of the man. The single glance, cold as flint.

'Budget class,' Hugo repeated, and the two words could have cut glass.

'That's…that's where she's from,' the conductor managed. 'I've searched her compartment and when I couldn't find the dog…'

'You searched my Amy's compartment?'

My Amy. She should be pleased, Amy thought.

Here he was, her hero, defending her. Instead…
My Amy. She felt like standing up and saying *Oi*!

But now was not a time for feminist principles.
Somehow she managed to subside. Her job was
to sit and look kissed.

That wasn't hard. She *was* kissed.

'She's brought the dog here,' the conductor said,
but instead of sounding sure, he was now sounding sulky and defensive. Henry the butler was
glancing at him as if he suspected he'd lost his
mind.

Woman coming to billionaire's bedroom at dead
of night—understandable. Woman smuggling dog
to billionaire's bed… Not so much.

But the conductor knew his job and was in-
tent on carrying it out. 'It's in there,' he said, and
pointed straight at Amy's purse. He darted forward—and then he hesitated. 'Does it bite?'

'Does what bite?' Hugo demanded, still at his
autocratic coldest.

'The dog.'

'You're saying a dog's in Miss Cotton's purse.'

'Yes.'

Hugo closed his eyes. He visibly counted to ten,
and then he opened them again.

He looked at Henry and hauteur gave way to sympathy. 'Are you okay with this?'

'Please…' said the miserable Henry. 'If you could just open the purse we could all just go back to…' he glanced at Amy '…to whatever we were doing.'

Indulge the lunatic and you'll be left alone, his tone said, and Hugo sighed and nodded.

'Okay. Let's do this. No, it won't bite,' he assured the conductor, and a commander approaching a shell-shocked soldier couldn't have achieved a more sympathetic tone. 'But let's make absolutely sure. Miss Cotton, would you open your purse for us?'

But Amy didn't move, or not instantly. Things were happening too fast—and she wasn't helped at all when, instead of handing her the purse, Hugo stooped and kissed her again, hard, fast, on the mouth.

'Sorry, love,' he told her. 'No. Don't move. I'll open it for you.' He grinned into her stunned eyes, patted her on the cheek—patted her!—and turned and opened the purse.

One book. Two magazines. Amy saw them through eyes that felt somehow blurry. Her world felt blurry.

But Hugo seemed unaware of her discombobulation. 'I believe Miss Cotton promised these to my grandmother,' he said gravely, pulling them out, laying them on the table and then turning the purse upside down and shaking it so they could all see a mouse-sized dog wasn't hiding in the lining. 'Plus a recipe she wanted. Amy hadn't…' his glance at Amy was pure wickedness '…she hadn't quite got round to emptying it before you gentlemen arrived. But not even the book is about dogs, so if you'll excuse us…'

'But it's here,' the conductor said, looking around wildly. 'It must be.'

Amy understood. This guy had his pride at stake. He'd pushed it this far. To back off now meant humiliation.

'Search, then,' Hugo said, with admirable patience and another sympathetic glance at Henry.

'She'll have hidden it in the bedroom,' the conductor said and darted towards the bedroom door.

Mistake. To say Hugo moved fast for a large man was an understatement.

In less than a millisecond Hugo's back was against Maud's bedroom door, and the unfortunate conductor was lifted right off the ground by his lapels.

'Enough,' Hugo growled, setting him down again and thrusting him backward with a force that had him staggering. His voice was low, obviously in deference to the sleeping Maud, but only a fool would ignore the threat his voice contained. 'I'll humour you here, in this sitting room, or even in my bedroom, but my grandmother is eighty-three years old, bereaved, exhausted and asleep.' He looked directly at Henry and his look was an order all by itself. 'If you wish to disturb my grandmother for this nonsense, it's on your head, but, I promise you, it will be your head.'

And Henry pulled himself together.

No matter how convincing his unfortunate underling—and underling the conductor must surely be, as denoted by the bars on his uniform—had been, Henry was no longer with him. Any belief in a hidden dog had long been dispelled.

He grabbed his companion's arm and hauled him away from Hugo.

'Out,' he ordered, appalled. 'Mr Thurston, we can't apologise enough. Miss Cotton...' he glanced at Amy '...Miss Cotton, we apologise to you as well. My colleague tells me you're leaving the train at Alice Springs and then rejoining on next week's run? Yes?' Then, as Amy found the strength for a feeble nod, he nodded back. There was a reason Henry was Platinum butler. He was collecting his authority around him as he spoke.

'Tomorrow, before you leave the train, I'll have arranged an upgrade to Platinum for your journey from Alice Springs to Darwin,' he said. 'I'd upgrade you tonight but your sister is already settled and you're busy…' He caught himself. 'I mean… you have other things to do tonight than change carriages. Please accept the humble apologies of myself and Albert. In mitigation, Albert had a report of a dog in the train. He needed to investigate, but I concede we've taken things too far. We won't be disturbing you further. Unless you'd like complimentary champagne? Strawberries?'

'We won't require anything else tonight,' Hugo said, motioning to the door back into the corridor. 'Just see that we're not disturbed again.'

'No, sir,' Henry said and practically shoved the unfortunate Albert out. 'Goodnight.'

'Goodnight,' Hugo said, and closed the door behind them.

He turned to Amy. He raised one quizzical eyebrow.

'My Amy?' she said. 'Oi!'

And then she started to laugh.

Hugo watched her laugh. She had her hands to her face. She was choking on laughter, choking on…

On what? This wasn't normal laughter.

He knelt before her and tugged her hands away from her face. He saw laughter, but something more. Something deeper?

She was on the edge, he thought, where laughter was close to tears, with hysteria close behind.

'No one's going to take your dog,' he said and tugged her into him and held.

For one long moment she resisted, but her body wasn't behaving. The laughter was sending spasms running through her and they made her powerless to resist. She crumpled against him and her body heaved as he held her.

'Sorry. It's not… It's just… I've been so worried about Rachel for so long, and tonight… You've been… You've been…'

'Heroic?' he suggested and she hiccuped on a laugh-cum-sob and subsided still more.

He held her. He just held.

She felt amazing. She was all silky pyjamas and fine blonde curls. Her hair was damp and smelled faintly citrusy. She'd just showered? She crumpled against his body and he thought he'd never felt anything, anyone like her.

She had a dancer's body. Not soft and curvy but tight, neat, every muscle knowing what it had to do. He could feel the latent strength in her, but right now she had no strength at all.

And something was twisting inside him. Something he didn't understand. For a woman to make him feel like this…

He didn't do emotion. When had he ever?

His mother's tears had been legion—hysterics, yelling, abuse, drama. This, though…

Her sister had smashed her pelvis. She'd lost her baby.

He thought back to Rachel's wan face and he wondered how much caring Amy had faced.

She'd told him that her sister had smiled on this trip for the first time since she'd lost the baby. All that time, Amy had been worrying?

The shuddering had eased. He figured she was trying to work out how to draw away without him seeing a face where laughter and tears had mixed.

He grimaced and hauled out a Thurston handkerchief. No commando in his right mind would be seen dead with a crisp linen handkerchief with a T embroidered in the corner but, from the moment he'd walked back into his grandmother's house, he'd had a Thurston handkerchief in his pocket. Right now he was grateful for it.

Amy, though, didn't appear to be grateful. The gesture was enough to pull her out of the emotional abyss she'd tumbled into. She pulled back and gazed down at the handkerchief in astonishment.

'You expect me to blow my nose on *this*?'

'It does seem a waste,' he admitted. 'But the option is?'

She handed the handkerchief back—and sniffed.

He grinned. 'That's my girl.'

'I am not your girl.' She glowered. 'Even if you are a hero. Do heroes carry handkerchiefs?'

'I don't expect they do.' He thought of the guys in his unit if they caught him with monogrammed handkerchiefs and the thought was enough to make him smile.

'And I don't normally cry.'

'You were laughing,' he agreed gravely. 'It just sort of got out of control.'

'It did.' She tugged back and tried to intensify the glower. 'You kissed me.'

'I did.' She really was beautiful, he thought.

She was ruffled and cute and tear-stained and she was fighting hard to be indignant. 'And very nice it was, too.'

'They'll think…'

'They did think, but there didn't seem a choice.' He tried to sound apologetic. 'What choice did we have? That you'd come the length of the train in your pyjamas to give me a recipe? Maybe not.'

She fought a bit longer to retain her glare but her gaze couldn't hold. She swallowed. 'Thank you,' she said finally, and it was almost a whisper.

'You don't need to thank me for kissing you. It was very, very nice.'

Indignation swelled again. 'Will you cut it out? And what have you done with my dog?'

His grandmother answered before he could. Maud's voice came from the doorway. 'He landed him on his grandma while he kissed you, that's what he did.'

They both turned and Maud was there, indignation personified. She was holding Buster in her arms and Buster was looking a bit indignant as well; he was having a very interrupted night's sleep.

'There I was,' Maud said, sighing with exasperation, 'almost asleep. Listening to the train wheels. Thinking, isn't this peaceful? And suddenly there's a dog under my bedclothes and Hugo whispering in a voice of doom, *"Keep him quiet, Maudie, or we'll all be tossed into the night"*. What sort of threat is that?' But her eyes were twinkling and Hugo thought, yes, mission accomplished—he had Maudie smiling again, too. Maudie and Amy both?

But Maudie was now looking at Amy and her gaze was turning thoughtful. Uh oh, he thought. Maudie back to normal was a force to be reckoned with.

'He's a useful man in a crisis, my Hugo,' she told Amy, and it was as if she was giving her grandson a reference. For a job she intended offering? 'You were wise to come to him.'

'Rescuing dogs and offering linen handkerchiefs…' Amy managed. 'As he said…very… heroic.'

'Aren't they lovely handkerchiefs?'

Maudie was in a neck to toe nightgown. Her white hair was flowing around her shoulders. She looked nothing like the immaculately coiffed Dame Maud the world knew, but she sounded as if she was having fun, and Hugo knew she was.

'I had them made by the hundred because James

always lost them,' she said. 'But now it's Hugo's role to keep up with the supply. I'm so glad he's sharing. And yes, you can blow your nose on it because he has hundreds more.'

Hmm, Hugo thought. She'd heard the nose blowing conversation. If so…how much else had she heard?

At her best, his grandmother missed nothing.

'Now,' Maud said sternly, advancing into the room and depositing Buster with Amy, 'much as I think this little dog is adorable, I need my beauty sleep and do you realise he snores? But Hugo's rescued him, so now he's Hugo's responsibility for the night. Meanwhile, I suggest you play Scrabble or anything else you can think of for a couple of hours…'

'I'm going to bed,' Amy said, looking startled.

'No, dear,' Maudie said severely. 'Not that it won't be nice eventually, for I think you're just the kind of girl Hugo needs, but not tonight. I know times have changed, but…'

'I mean in *my* bed,' Amy said, beginning to look appalled. 'You know very well that I do.'

'Yes, dear,' Maudie said. 'Though…'

'Though nothing,' Amy said firmly. 'My bed it is. But Buster…' she faltered '…I guess…'

'Exactly,' Maudie said and her smile widened. 'I heard those two men out in the corridor. Henry's not looking for dogs any more, but the man from your carriage is far from convinced. If you scuttle back…'

'I do not scuttle,' Amy said indignantly.

'You could if you needed to,' Hugo volunteered. 'I bet you could. If you can dance you can scuttle.'

'Be quiet, Hugo,' Maudie said. 'You've done very well up till now, but it takes a woman's brain to see this through. Amy, you've come here for a rendezvous with my grandson so a rendezvous you will have. Only, of course, as you said, you're a good girl so you won't stay the night. Two hours of Scrabble should do it. Then you'll settle Buster into Hugo's bed and you'll take your empty purse back to your cabin. Hugo, you'll escort her. I don't want Amy wandering the train in her pyjamas, whatever she's done up until now.'

'But…' said Amy.

'Hush,' Maudie told her. 'Just listen. Hugo, you'll keep Buster until morning; it'd be asking for trouble for Amy to carry him back to her cabin. Then tomorrow, Amy, you and your sister will come back here—carrying your purse again. Make it bulge with books again. We'll have breakfast together in this sitting room. We'll spend the morning together until we get into Alice Springs and then we'll take it from there. Any objections?'

'But...' said Amy again. She couldn't seem to get past that.

'Maudie...' Hugo started.

But Maudie was already retreating. 'That's settled,' she said. 'If there are no more rescues to be effected, I'm off to bed. Goodnight to you both.'

And she giggled and closed the door behind her.

Leaving Hugo looking at Amy. And dog.

What to do with a woman in pink satin pyjamas for two hours?

If she was another sort of woman...

She wasn't.

There were three types of women in the world of Hugo Thurston.

There were the women like his mother. His mother had married his father because he was a Thurston, and she'd revelled in the money, fame and glamour. The media/fame thing had become an addiction, as had alcohol, drugs and crazy cosmetic surgery, until they'd taken their final terrible toll.

With his family background, with the money he knew he'd inherit even before his father had died, there'd always been women like his mother wanting to be seen with him. He avoided them like the plague.

Then there were the women he worked with—colleagues, friends, women who treated him as a soldier and who didn't get the Thurston thing. They were a tough breed, and they were the only women he was comfortable with. Occasionally he'd get close to one of them, but his work meant he moved around. Relationships were transient and these women knew his world.

Somehow his grandmother fitted into this category, too, he thought. She'd fought side by side with his grandfather to build their empire, and she'd learned the rules from the ground up. Outside the army, though, the chances of finding another Maud were zero.

Those two categories were the women he knew how to deal with: women who understood his army life, and women who courted the media.

Then there were 'normal' women, those who didn't know the army world and who didn't know the Thurston world. Asking someone not in the military to understand the dangers of his job, to live with not knowing where he was, what he was doing, to ask her to live with his nightmares, his world, when he couldn't explain… Such a relationship would be impossible and he'd never attempt it. Nor could he ever ask someone unfamiliar with it to cope with the media hype of the Thurston world.

And Amy was normal, he thought. She was small, blonde and cute. She came across as vulnerable. She was definitely in the third category—not of his world.

So it had been a bad idea to kiss her—he knew it had—but he looked down at her now and he really badly wanted to kiss her again.

'Don't even think about it,' she growled and he took a step back.

'About what?'

'You know very well what.'

Was he that obvious? Maybe he was. He was in a tiny sitting room with a beautiful woman in lacy satin pyjamas. Maybe it'd take a stronger man than him not to be obvious.

'I don't think…' he started.

'Excellent. Don't think, except what letters you have in front of you. Scrabble. Is this your position or your grandmother's?'

'Mine.'

'You're losing.'

'Story of my life,' he said. 'So you won't kiss me again?'

'No.'

'Can I ask why not?' Of all the dumb questions… Where was he going with this?

And she didn't know, either. She was looking at him as if he had a kangaroo loose in the top paddock—which pretty much summed up how he was feeling.

And, as if she knew best lunatic practice, she relented and explained simply, in words even a lunatic could understand.

'One,' she said, patience personified. 'I'm not a one-night stand sort of girl. I may have been desperate enough to lurch in here with my dog and my pyjamas, but I'm still respectable. So if you're thinking of pushing it, don't. Your grandma's right through that door and I know enough of Dame Maud to bet one scream will have you chastised like you're six years old. You may look like a warrior but you're a warrior with a grandma. I'm prepared to use her kindness as a human shield.'

'Right,' he said faintly. 'And two?'

'Two? Two is that I'm not interested in any sort of relationship. What Dame Maud was suggesting… No. If you're thinking one kiss could signal the beginning of an affair, even a tiddly, inconspicuous affair, I'll tell you where to put that as well.'

'Can I ask why?' He shouldn't ask—this was the craziest of conversations—but she had him intrigued.

'Because, even though you're drop-dead gorgeous, and even though the tabloids have you as a billionaire and your grandpa's heir, and you even say you're hero material, I'm totally, absolutely not in the market for any sort of relationship. It's taken me months to persuade Rachel to come away with me. You think two days into our journey I'm going to turn around and say, "Sorry, Rachel, go back to your books for a while because I have this hot guy in Car Two"?'

'I understand,' he said, and did, but what he didn't understand was his unfathomable sense of loss.

There was an attraction between them. She'd felt it—she must have felt it. He'd intended that kiss to be fast and hot and leave her flustered enough to look…well, flustered. What he hadn't counted on was that it had left him feeling as he'd intended her to look.

As if he'd been interrupted in the midst of something vital to them both.

'Scrabble,' she said, and started checking her squares. 'Sit. Play.'

'Yes, ma'am,' he said and sat and played, and if neither of them found a word that'd make either Rachel or Maud proud...well, what was to be expected when neither of their minds were on Scrabble?

CHAPTER FOUR

Two hours later they decided even Amy's conductor would be convinced they'd had enough time to have a red-hot liaison. They'd certainly run out of Scrabble options.

There were lots of things Amy would have liked to ask this guy. He'd been in the army since he was seventeen. He'd travelled in some of the most amazing countries in the world and she'd never been out of Australia. She would have loved to ask him…lots.

But there was something about Hugo Thurston that stopped her asking anything, and he very carefully didn't ask her anything back.

After five games of Scrabble, Amy was one to Hugo's four, she was pretty much close to screaming and thankfully it was time for her to go back to Car Six.

She settled Buster into Hugo's bed and told him to stay. During Rachel's marriage, the little dog had become accustomed to being left with friends while Amy was performing. He was a handbag dog and he made no demur when she left him. In fact, he looked as if he kind of liked Hugo's man-sized bed.

Why not? It was better than the narrow bunk she was going back to, she thought, but she shoved the thought aside—and then thought: hooray, thanks to this night she'd be travelling Platinum on the next leg. That was a thought to cheer a girl up. She headed out into the corridor—and Hugo came with her.

'There's no need to take me home,' she said a trifle breathlessly. Just being near this guy made her breathless.

'Maud's orders,' he said simply. 'I'm a man who follows orders.'

'Scared of your grandma?'

'All of my life.'

'I don't believe you.'

'I don't tell lies.'

'Says the man who dusted dog hairs out of my purse.'

'Shush.' They were approaching the butler's pantry but the door was closed. Hopefully, Henry was fast asleep.

'No one's awake,' she said. 'And I don't need company.'

'What if there's a camel and no Buster to protect you?'

She smiled and kept going, but she didn't feel like smiling. In truth she was feeling totally… disconcerted. The last few hours had been weird enough, but now, making her way through the jolting, rumbling train, with this really disconcerting guy right behind her…

What was it about this guy that made him… disconcerting?

The train rolled a little and she stumbled. He was right behind, and he caught her shoulders and steadied her.

More disconcerting. Really, really disconcerting.

The train steadied and so did she. Sort of. She set off again, feeling ridiculous, absurdly aware of the warrior behind her, ready to catch her if she stumbled. Woman in pink satin being escorted home by her own personal bodyguard.

No one was awake. Thanks be. One foot after another, she told herself, and ignore the bodyguard.

Not possible.

She reached the door of her compartment and turned and he was even more impossible to ignore.

He was far too near for comfort. He hadn't done his shirt buttons up since that crazy interlude with the train staff. She'd noticed those undone buttons. Of course she had. Maybe that was why she'd lost at Scrabble. Once or twice she'd thought about asking him to do them up—as she'd done hers up really fast the moment the train staff had left. He hadn't, though, and she wished…

Or maybe she didn't wish. Maybe she had no idea any more what she was wishing.

'Thank you and goodnight,' she managed, and she couldn't stop herself sounding breathless. Like an overawed teenager. 'You've been…very good.'

'I have, haven't I,' he said gravely. 'Is Maud right? Does Buster snore?'

'He dreams,' she admitted. 'When he does, he wuffles.'

'If he has nightmares, should I fetch you?'

'No!'

'No?' he said and grinned. 'You're condemning me to sharing my bed with nightmares.'

'You look big enough to cope.'

'I am,' he said, and his smile faded. 'I'm big

enough to cope with anything.' His smile had suddenly disappeared.

Nightmares.

She thought suddenly that this man had almost twenty years in the army, in a unit she knew of only by its fearsome reputation. What nightmares were there? She knew by his face that the word had conjured up images that appalled. And even before the armed forces? She knew enough of his parents to think there'd have been nightmares for Hugo Thurston since birth.

Maybe the warrior thing was out of place. She looked up at him and was hit by an almost irresistible urge to…to…

The train jerked again and his hands once more caught her shoulders. She felt herself fall against him.

Accidentally?

Maybe not so much.

His hands felt amazing. His chest felt amazing, and if she just tilted her chin…

Her chin tilted all by itself as she searched his face. His eyes were grave and questioning, and she felt…

Exposed. A flashlight, from so close…

The door to the next compartment had opened.

It was the guy who'd yelled about the dog, and he was holding his phone as a camera.

The door of his compartment slammed behind him and he was gone almost before she knew he'd been there. And Hugo had let her go and was shoving the guy's closed door.

It was locked. Of course it was locked. Amy had glimpsed the guy's face—he'd looked excited but he'd also looked scared.

Hugo thumped on the door. Nothing. He raised his fist to thump again but Amy grabbed his arm.

'No! Do you want to wake the whole car?'

'If that photo…'

'If he wakes the car, we'll have the whole train seeing me here in my pyjamas. Ask him to delete it in the morning.'

'Amy…'

'It doesn't matter,' she said wearily. 'He'll be the one who reported the dog. Maybe that's what he was doing—waiting for me to come back with a dog. Well, he didn't see a dog, and if some perv wants to take photos… We weren't even actually kissing. Just close.'

She laid her hand on his arm, wanting to dispel the anger, the flash of darkness across his features. Once again came that insight, the certainty that there'd been nightmares in this guy's past and they were with him still. 'Hugo, let it go,' she said, gently now. 'I need to go to bed. You need to go back to Buster. It's a whole new day tomorrow and we don't need to spoil it by creating World War Three now.'

He looked furious. Frustrated. A coiled spring...

She glanced out of the window, trying to think of something that'd dispel that black look. 'There are lights out there,' she said. 'Wow, this is practically a city.'

They were indeed going through a settlement. She counted a whole six lights.

'It's a wonder we don't stop to shop,' she said, still struggling to reach him. 'Do you think we should pull the emergency cord? I haven't bought a souvenir yet, on this whole trip.'

'You'd need to consider the way you're dressed before pulling the cord,' he said, his grim look fading a little as he reluctantly moved on. 'You won't get the respect you need when you face a sales assistant in pyjamas.'

'There is that,' she said ruefully, and she looked up into his face and saw all sorts of tensions she couldn't hope to understand. 'It's okay,' she said softly. 'There's no war zone here. Relax. We'll talk to the guy with the phone in the morning. Now, off you go and sleep with Buster. There's an offer impossible to resist.'

And then, because she couldn't help herself, before she even knew she'd intended it, because the grim look was still there and she couldn't bear it, she stood on tiptoe and she kissed him lightly on the lips.

It was a feather kiss of thanks, of reassurance, of goodnight. That was all it was, and then she tugged the door open behind her and backed into her compartment.

'Thank you,' she said softly. 'You truly are a hero. Thank you, Hugo, for saving my skin. I'd hate to be out there with the camels.'

'Even with a shopping opportunity?' He was trying to smile.

She smiled back at him. Then she backed into her compartment and closed the door behind her.

He waited in the corridor until he was sure she wasn't coming out again. He stood, silent, waiting, as he'd stood and waited and watched in so many dangerous places in the world.

Then, softly, he knocked on the compartment door of the guy who'd taken the picture.

No answer.

'Mr Murcott, you know who I am,' Hugo said, almost pleasantly. But quietly. Amy didn't want the whole carriage woken and he'd respect her wishes. To a point. 'You know the power I wield,' he added. 'Will you open the door or do I need to take it off its hinges?'

He waited. Finally the door opened and Hugo was face to face with the guy he'd endured during lunch. The man was wearing blue flannelette pyjamas. He was middle aged, flabby, florid— and wearing pyjamas wasn't a good look. His wife was in the bottom bunk with her bedclothes hauled up round her neck, looking terrified.

'He got rid of it,' she said before Hugo could say a word. 'He deleted it. I said to him, "Roger", I said…'

'Let me see,' Hugo said and held out his hand.

The guy handed over his phone. Hugo knew this model. Top of the range. Capable of taking a high resolution photograph.

He flicked through to the end of the photo file and saw endless pictures of train and desert and of the meals they'd had. Boring.

Nothing else.

'When Roger told me what he'd seen out there,

I said you wouldn't like it,' the woman volunteered. She seemed a mixture of virtue and terror. 'I said quick, get rid of it. I said Mr Thurston would be angry.'

He stared at them both. They gazed back and the terror was palpable.

They were too terrified, he thought. Why?

He turned and gazed out of the window. Blackness. Nothing and nothing and nothing.

The bars on the guy's phone showed no reception.

'You sent it,' he said, his voice lowering even further.

'How could we send it?' It was still the woman doing the talking. 'As if we would.'

'If it's been sent…'

'We don't understand email anyway,' Roger whined and Hugo knew that he did.

The Internet was out there, vast and all consuming. Somewhere…a photo.

What could be achieved by threatening the guy?

'You do know the power I possess,' he said, deciding that being a Thurston had to be useful for something. 'If I find that photo's been distributed in any way…you have no idea of the things I can arrange to have happen.'

Neither did he, he thought ruefully, but that was beside the point. The couple paled, as if he'd promised his SWAT team would be waiting at the next stop with a torture chamber on the back of a camel. He could have smiled if he wasn't so worried. That photo…

'We haven't sent it. We couldn't send it even if we wanted to,' Roger was bleating. 'There's no reception out here. And the photo's been deleted. Don't worry, Mr Thurston. And we won't tell anyone what just happened. You can rely on us to be discreet.'

I bet I can't, Hugo thought, but there was nothing else he could do. The photo was no longer on the guy's phone. If he had managed to send it, all he could hope was that it ended up somewhere innocuous and his threats meant it wouldn't be taken further.

There was nothing else he could do.

He closed the door without bothering to say anything more and then headed back to his carriage.

Past Amy's compartment.

He'd like to…

No. He had too much sense to like anything of the sort.

Bed. With Buster.

CHAPTER FIVE

RACHEL and Amy had breakfast in Platinum with
Maud and Hugo. And Buster. Buster sat on Maud's
knee and ate bacon. They retreated to their own
compartment for the rest of the journey, but when
the train pulled into Alice Springs Maud was already organising their transport.

Saying no to Maud was like saying no to a tor-
nado. It had no effect whatsoever. And besides,
she wasn't taking over their lives; she was simply
making their lives easier.

'I know you have a bus booked to take you
to Uluru but it's a five-hour drive and how can
Buster put up with that?'

'We'll have rest stops,' Amy said, but she already knew she was beaten. People were piling
onto buses. Lots of people. Closer to the platform,
a sleek silver Mercedes was parked in priority
parking. The guy who'd delivered it had handed
the keys to Hugo as if Hugo was his boss. With
deference.

Amy noticed, as she was noticing everything about this man. She was trying hard not to notice but internally orders were being disobeyed all over the place.

Right now Hugo was lifting his grandmother's luggage into the trunk, waiting for Maud to win the argument. Rachel seemed passive. Buster didn't care and Amy's only argument as to why they shouldn't accept a lift with Hugo and his grandmother was all about how she was noticing Hugo. And how she couldn't stop noticing.

He looked great, she thought. He was in jeans and a white T-shirt, and the T-shirt was stretched a bit too tight. The sun was glinting on his hair. His bronzed skin fitted in with the landscape here as if he was a local, and he was stowing luggage as if he were readying for action.

An outback warrior. She wasn't staying with him. No way.

'I'm not insisting on you staying with us,' Maud said gently, as if reading her thoughts. 'I know you like your independence. All I'm offering is a car ride instead of a bus. Your sister's hip hurts, I know it does. And the little dog would be much happier. Rachel?'

And, astonishingly, Rachel responded.

'My hip does hurt,' she told Amy, sounding apologetic. 'It'd be lovely to go by car rather than bus.'

And she flashed Amy a look that was almost speculative. *Et tu, Brute?* Amy thought. If Rachel started matchmaking, too…

No. She was imagining things. This was sensible, for all of them. It was nothing to do with what was between Hugo and Amy.

'Thank you,' Amy said, trying to sound gracious instead of trapped. 'That'll be lovely.'

'Excellent,' Maudie said and beamed. 'Hugo's ordered food for the trip and he's ordered for four. We knew you'd see sense. Now let Hugo put your gear into the car, then you, Amy, pop into the front beside Hugo, and Rachel and I will have a wee nap in the back.'

'Maud…' Hugo said warningly.

'Yes, dear?' She was all innocence.

'You're sitting up front with me,' Hugo said. 'Amy and Rachel are in the back. Quit it with the conniving. Neither Amy nor I are interested.'

And Amy blushed.

Up until now she'd never blushed in her life. She didn't think she could.

Her imagination wasn't playing tricks. Maud was matchmaking. She definitely blushed.

They settled into the Mercedes and headed south for the five-hour drive to Uluru. The car was beautiful, a sleek Mercedes that ate the miles while they sat in comfort. Or slept in comfort. Maud napped and so did Rachel.

Rachel had finally relaxed, Amy thought. This morning she'd seemed almost eager to have breakfast with Hugo and Maud, and amazingly she'd wanted to drive to Uluru with them. The Rachel of a week ago would have cringed and demanded the anonymity of a seat as far in the back of a bus as she could get. Somehow, Maud's presence was making her relax, giving her something Amy hadn't been able to provide.

A grandma?

Maybe that was it, Amy thought.

Their parents had been… Well, *parents* probably didn't describe the pair who'd produced Amy and Rachel. Dianne had been wild and passionate and what she'd been most passionate about was her freedom. She'd coupled briefly with a guitar-toting surfer. They'd travelled through Australia, had a couple of kids on the way, then tired of them. Amy and Rachel had been one and three when Dianne dumped them on her mother, and she'd never come back.

It didn't matter. They were happier and healthier with their grandma. Bess had raised them with all the love she knew how, and her death when Amy was twelve and Rachel was ten was a fierce, aching loss.

When Dianne died of a drug overdose three years later the girls felt nothing, and heaven alone knew where their father was. When Bess died, when the girls were desperate for support, Social Services tried to contact him, but obviously fatherhood wasn't his scene.

They didn't need anyone else, they'd told each other, but they'd ached for their Grandma Bess, for her stories, for her sense of family, and here, now, Rachel was relaxing in the company of another grandma. Maud made Rachel smile, and the sensation for Amy was indescribable. Someone was lifting a weight from her shoulders.

But it wasn't only Maud doing the lifting. She glanced at Hugo's broad shoulders as he drove and, despite the sheer sexual awareness she was trying to ignore, she was aware of a wash of gratitude.

How many grandsons would take this sort of journey with their grandmothers? How many men would care as he so obviously cared for Maud?

He was a soldier. After this journey…would he be heading back to harm's way?

The thought was suddenly heavy. She thought of what she'd read about this man, about the empire he could now head. It was so big it'd run itself, she thought. Sir James and Dame Maud had always kept a personal interest but, with James's death and Maud's increasing age, the Thurston empire could become just another international conglomerate.

But…the Thurston empire was worth more than that. It had a reputation for social justice but, for that to keep happening, Hugo would need to step in as head. His life would have to change.

She watched the set of his shoulders and she thought that was what he was facing. Time to stop the soldiering and come home?

Why not? Wasn't it time he stopped with the nightmares? Whatever the nightmares were. She could only imagine.

Whoa, this was so none of her business. She had no business wanting to hug this guy, to rid him of demons. Instead, she hugged Buster and concentrated on the scenery: vast red-dirt country, wild, untrammelled and wonderful.

They were approaching a river—the Finke, the sign said, and she gazed at the riverbed in wonder.

Apart from a few waterholes glistening in the afternoon sun, the river was dry, but it looked as if a great swathe of water had just rushed through, washing the sandy riverbed clean. There were rivulets, ripples and gashes in the sand, making the riverbed look like surreal modern art.

It was weird and beautiful, and when Hugo slowed and parked she kept right on gazing.

'It's fantastic, isn't it,' Hugo said, not turning, speaking softly, and she knew it was to her alone. Maud and Rachel were deeply asleep. Maybe they should wake them—but for both of them sleep meant healing and there was no way they'd interfere.

'It's magic,' Amy breathed. 'Have you seen this before?'

'My grandfather brought me here. You need to come just after the wet season to see it like this. It's my favourite time.'

They sat, he in the front, she in the back, and simply watched the great swathe of washed sand.

An eagle came swooping from nowhere and

swept along the vast length of riverbed, searching for his dinner or simply loving the arid beauty of the place.

She was growing fanciful, Amy thought. They should keep going—they still had three hours' driving ahead of them—but when Hugo said 'Would you like to get out?' she was out of the car almost before he'd finished saying it.

She walked from the bridge to the riverbed, carrying Buster, and Hugo followed silently behind.

He wasn't a talker, she thought. He was a big, silent man who watched from the sidelines and took action when needed.

He felt…

She felt…

She didn't actually know how she felt. All she knew was that she was grateful for this moment, for being here now—and for the fact that he was here with her.

She reached the washed sand and set Buster down. Buster sniffed, raised his head and looked along the pristine riverbed—and then something extraordinary happened.

He sniffed the sand at his feet and then sniffed again. His ears pricked straight up and his tail went rigid behind him. He raised one paw and stood motionless, in the stance of the great hunting dogs of old.

He was a frail fox terrier, with the adventures of his youth far behind him. He was a little bit lame. Barking at the camels on the train had been about as exciting as life ever got for Buster; as exciting as he ever wanted it to get. For the last few years, when Amy took him to the park, his perambulations had become more and more sedate.

Here, though… Here there were smells he didn't recognise. Here were sights that stirred something deep inside, and they were stirred. One small domestic dog put his face into the wind, gave one ecstatic bark and then ran.

He flew down the riverbed so fast, so far that Amy took fright and called after him, but he wasn't out of control, he wasn't leaving. Just as he reached the point where she might have panicked, he wheeled and came back to her, but not in a straight line. He raced in wide, wild loops, again and again, his small paws making crazy circles on the pristine sand.

He had a gammy leg but he wasn't noticing. He looked wild and free and happy, and Amy's heart felt…felt… What?

Hugo was standing beside her. She clutched his arm and held.

These last two years had been awful. It had been Amy who'd introduced Rachel to the ghastly Ramón, but who'd have thought, who'd ever have known that behind the loving, charming smile lay a self-absorbed bully? Rachel had kept the darkness of her marriage secret, or she'd tried to, but Amy had seen her once-bubbly sister grow quieter and quieter. Then, when the smash came…

Rachel had almost died and Ramón didn't care. He'd twisted an ankle, torn a ligament. It threatened to derail his dancing, and the loss of his baby daughter was nothing in comparison.

It was Amy who had to do the caring. It was Amy who had to walk away from her ballet.

She'd had little choice. She could no longer dance near Ramón without wanting to commit murder, and her practice commitments left Rachel alone for far too long. She tried to be practical. Her body was wearying—she'd need to leave eventually—so she let Rachel think her trifling ills were worse than they were. But, as the months wore on, her sister's bleakness had become a black hole that threatened to engulf them both.

There were worse things to survive than ceasing dancing, she'd told herself over and over, and the job she was heading for in Darwin sounded lovely. But here, now…instead of a job that might cheer her in the future, she was nearing her grandmother's birthplace, somewhere she and Rachel had dreamed of visiting for ever—and, what was even better, she had a dog practically doing cartwheels on the riverbed *right now*. The sun was on her face, her sister was happy and she was laughing and cheering—and Hugo's arm came around her and held her, and she thought, right at this moment, this was heaven.

'He hardly ever even puts his gammy leg down,' she breathed. 'Oh, Hugo… Oh, we might have gone on the bus. Oh, thank you.'

'Think nothing of it,' Hugo said in an odd voice and she glanced up at him and saw that he wasn't watching her dog. He was watching her.

'So the smuggling paid off?' he asked, still in that odd voice. She should step back. She was way too close. Instead, she twisted in his hold so she was in his clasp, facing him, and his arms were around her waist.

In the hold of lovers?

No, she thought, feeling weirdly desperate. The hold of friends. This guy could be a friend.

He already was.

'Crime pays,' she managed and he smiled and his smile took her breath away. To have such a man smile at her as Hugo was smiling at her, right here, right now…

She wanted to do the odd cartwheel herself.

Maybe…maybe…

But then Buster came flying back, quivering in every inch of his body. He nosed her leg and Hugo laughed and released her and she felt an absurd sense of loss.

No matter. He was a friend, she told herself fiercely. Men and women could be friends. They could.

'Friends,' Hugo said, and she glanced up at him sharply. Was he thinking the same as she was? He'd used the word almost as a defence.

Great. If the two of them were feeling this tug…

Not possible. He was an awesome guy. For him to think of her as anything but a friend…

He was a friend. He'd just said so.

'Accomplice in crime,' she managed. 'I go down, you go down.'

'Thanks very much.'

He grinned and her feeling of light returned.

Buster started doing his crazy loop thing again and she couldn't help herself.

She stepped a little away from Hugo, put her hands down on the sun-warmed sand and did a cartwheel herself. And then another.

She was wearing a light cotton T-shirt over her leggings. Travelling gear. Practice gear.

She hadn't danced for months. That last day, she'd gone into rehearsal and Ramón had been there, smug, arrogant, being charming to one of the new girls.

She was tired and angry and she'd had enough. She'd walked out and hadn't been back. She hadn't danced since, but now, here, her body seemed to dance all on its own. The sun on her face, her dog, this place…

Hugo.

He was a friend, she thought, nothing more, and a friend wouldn't mind if she went a little bit nuts. So she turned half a dozen cartwheels and then, as Buster barked hysterically, she spun and spun and spun until the world spun with her and nothing mattered except this moment and the sunshine and the desert and Hugo's smile…

And when she finally ceased, dizzy with happiness, he caught her and held her and he laughed as if he felt as free and as wonderful as she did. She heard clapping from the bank and looked up and Rachel and Maudie were cheering and clapping at them both.

And Hugo still held her.

He was a friend. With a friend like this…

'Sandwiches,' Maudie called from the bank. 'I'm hungry. Is this intermission or curtain call?'

Rachel was standing beside her. They were both grinning. Rachel stooped and called Buster. Buster did a couple more crazy loop-runs then stopped, looked about him, seemed to gather himself, remembered that he had a gammy leg and then limped bravely up the bank towards sandwiches.

They all laughed.

Hugo linked his hand in hers and they walked together back to the car and Amy felt…as if the sand under her feet was shifting and she didn't have a clue what was underneath.

'Let's go,' he said, and she thought: I don't actually know where I'm going.

He kept on driving. Beside him Maud chattered and gossiped and the two women in the back seat joined in, but Hugo wasn't joining in.

Why had he done…what he'd done?

What had he done?

He'd held hands with a woman as she'd walked up the riverbank. He'd laughed with her. He'd hugged her.

Why wouldn't he hug her? She was adorable.

She was also out of bounds.

He did not do relationships with vulnerable women who could be destroyed in his world. Who *would* be destroyed in his world.

What was his world? Back on the battlefields of Afghanistan, or taking his grandfather's place as head of Thurston Holdings?

What he was doing overseas now was crucial. He was training the locals to fight their own battles, to keep the peace.

It could be done by others. Heading Thurston Holdings, though…running the company as his grandfather had expected it to be run… Who could that be done by?

No one but him.

His conscience told him there was no way out, but what it entailed… The guy taking photographs back there on the train was the tip of the iceberg. He did not want to live under the glare of media scrutiny.

He might not have a choice—but he was *not* going to haul a woman into it as well.

A woman like Amy?

She looked…fragile, he thought. Neat and compact and small.

He thought suddenly of a lovely old music box of his grandmother's. When she lifted the lid, a tiny, fragile dancer whirled to gentle music, and she'd let him play with it as a child.

'Close the lid gently,' his grandmother always said. 'You don't want to hurt her.'

Amy was a ballerina. She had nothing to do with soldiering. She'd never been faced with an aggressive and intrusive media.

He glanced in the rear view mirror and watched her. She was laughing at something Maud said. He should have been listening.

He very carefully hadn't been listening. *In dangerous situations don't allow yourself to become emotionally involved. No matter what the urge, resist until the area's safe.*

Amy was laughing.

The area wasn't safe. This was a minefield and he was walking right through it.

Close the lid of the music box and walk away.

* * *

The moment they reached the hostel Amy and Rachel had booked, Amy knew she was in trouble.

There was nothing wrong with the place. It looked clean, welcoming and fun—only that was the problem. Fun. The moment they arrived, scores of young men and women surrounded their car.

'Welcome!' someone called. 'You're just in time for the barbecue. Did you bring booze?'

'First drink's on us,' someone else yelled. 'But, seeing you have a car… We're in danger of running dry. Take pity on us, please.'

There were cheers and laughter and entreaties in a dozen different accents.

Uh oh.

If I was nineteen and not responsible for a recovering Rachel and a hidden dog I might look at this place with delight, Amy thought. But, as it was…

'You're not staying here,' Maud stated, imperious in her decisiveness. Rachel clutched her hand, rigid with tension, and Amy knew the sensible thing would be to accept Maud's offer.

Why didn't she want to stay with Hugo?

For the same reason he wasn't saying anything

now. For the same reason he glanced at her and looked away fast. There was this *thing* between them. This indefinable thing. They both knew it was there. They could feel it. It was tangible, real.

It was real and it was dangerous.

Staying in the same house as him for the next few days would be crazy. But…

'Maud, is it okay if we stay with you?' Rachel was saying. 'I want to.'

Uh oh, indeed. This was the first definite decision she'd heard from Rachel since the accident.

What to do?

She could tell Rachel to shut up—or she could let things happen.

She glanced at Hugo. Could she let things happen without…things happening?

What was she thinking? Of course she could. She'd danced in the tight community of a ballet company for years. During rehearsals and performance, dancers lived in a hotbed of emotional tension. Relationships flared, erupted, ended. She'd learned to stay aloof, so all she needed to do was stay aloof for the next few days.

While she stayed in Hugo's house.

Maud's house. She was staying with Maud, not Hugo. Hugo would simply be a guy on the periphery.

Except she looked at Hugo and she thought this wasn't a guy who was on the periphery of anything.

They accepted Maud's very gracious offer. Hugo turned the car south—and looming before them was Uluru. Ayers Rock. It was still over ten miles away but it was still the most amazing sight Amy had ever seen.

'Stop,' she breathed.

Hugo obligingly stopped.

It was after dark. Amy hadn't expected to see anything of the rock tonight but the moon had risen, a great tangerine ball lighting the desert. The horizon was stark and endless, and the rock rose from the darkness like the vast, ancient monolith it was.

She and Rachel had dreamed of seeing this for so long, and now to be here... The place their grandmother had talked of. Their dreaming place.

She could scarcely believe it.

'It feels like coming home,' Rachel whispered and Amy thought she was right. Home.

Their childhood home had been rented rooms, poverty, anywhere Bess could afford to keep her granddaughters in the bleakness of a vast city.

After Bess's death there'd been foster homes. For Amy, home—of sorts—had then become the ballet and, for Rachel, university. But for all the time, for both of them, in the background had been the thought of this place, their grandmother's home. A rock, a place—but so much more.

The concept of belonging?

Walking away from the ballet had been gut-wrenching. What Rachel had been through was worse.

Somehow the thought of this place had seemed a kind of answer.

'Did your family come from here?' Hugo asked softly into the night, and Amy managed to nod. For some absurd reason, it seemed right that Hugo was here with her. The thought was unsettling—the man was unsettling—but she needed to find him an answer.

'Our grandma was born here,' she said, trying to sound prosaic. 'She left as a kid, sent away to school and never got back. Coming here seems like doing it for her.'

'I'm glad,' Hugo said simply and disappeared into the background and let them be.

No explanation. No fuss. He'd simply retreated from this most personal of moments. Inexplicably,

Amy's heart twisted. She should be totally focused on the rock, but something had just happened. Some shift in the way she felt.

Why?

She didn't know.

What she was feeling for Hugo was surely a transitory weakness, she told herself. Here, in this place, surely she should vow to put such feelings away, to focus on what was important.

But what was important?

Inevitably, it was Maud who told her.

'Buster's getting restless,' she called from the car. 'Does he need to pee?'

That was important, Amy told herself as she turned to take care of her dog. Practicalities—and not falling into the emotional abyss Rachel had suffered.

But the way she was feeling about Hugo…

He was a Thurston, she told herself. He was also a soldier. There was no future for her in either of those parts of his life, so she might as well school herself now.

To do what? Not to…feel?

How many days until the next train?

* * *

The hostel Amy had chosen had been basic. The Thurston house wasn't. They pulled into the driveway and Amy could only gaze in wonder. From arid desert, they'd suddenly entered a green and lush oasis.

'What is this place?' she breathed.

'Thurstons' mines are south of here,' Hugo told them. 'But Grandpa loved this place, so when he negotiated for mining rights he also negotiated to build this. It's supposedly a base for his mine managers but in truth it's his and Maud's personal refuge.'

'But it looks…'

'Like an over-the-top homestead?' He grinned. 'It's surely that. There's an underground spring so we can have a garden. Grandpa planted almost every indigenous plant that'll live here. In the morning you'll see wildlife—everything in a hundred mile radius makes use of this garden and waterhole. Meanwhile, come inside and see if we come up to the same standard as your backpackers' hostel.'

There was never any doubt that it did.

The homestead was built on classic lines, long and low, with a wide veranda running its length. The garden seemed to merge seamlessly with the veranda. Long French windows were open, their curtains fluttering outward, the lights on and welcoming.

'Does anyone live here?' Amy breathed.

'Scott and Wendy have their own house out the back,' Maud said, beaming at her reaction. 'Scott looks after the grounds and Wendy's the housekeeper.'

'They know we're coming,' Hugo told them. 'I told them there was a possibility of two more, so the beds will be ready. Welcome to Natangarra.'

And he flung the doors wide and the house welcomed them inside.

Wow.

This was what it was to be seriously rich, Amy thought. To have a place like this, on call, whenever you needed it…

'There's a swimming pool,' Rachel breathed, looking through into the internal courtyard.

'We needed to build it inside,' Maud said. 'Otherwise we'd have kangaroos fighting for swimming rights. But we have a magnificent waterhole out the back—you'll be able to see it in the morning. No animal goes thirsty here. Now, what do you girls want to do while you're here?'

Stay here, Amy thought, feeling stunned. Sit by

this swimming pool and stop. Let someone else worry about Rachel for a change.

She and Rachel had just the one thing they must do…and, to her astonishment, Rachel was being proactive about it.

'I want to walk around Uluru,' she said. 'I won't be able to get all the way but I'd like to try. And…and there's something we need to do there. Something private. Then I'm sending Amy out for rock samples.' She suddenly looked doubtful. 'But we planned this from the resort. We had bus tickets.'

'That's what Hugo's here for,' Maud said and beamed. 'He needs excitement.'

'Driving us round the country is hardly exciting,' Amy said, glancing at Hugo and thinking the guy looked hunted. As well he might. But she didn't feel too sorry for him. She glanced through to the magnificent living room, with its vast squishy sofas, its ceiling fans, its gorgeous air of faded comfort. This house was huge and the property must be just as vast. Bossy grandma or not, the man had serious compensations.

'Do you have a spare vehicle?' she asked. 'A farm truck or something I could borrow? That'd make Rachel and me independent.'

Hugo's face cleared. 'Of course…'

'Nonsense,' Maud said briskly. 'It'll do you good to play chauffeur. You've been bored to death with just your grandmother to take care of. Now…supper and bed. In the morning Hugo can take you to the base of Uluru. We'll work out the rest of the itinerary from there. We have four days, and we must make the most of them.'

'Aren't you staying longer?' Amy ventured. 'I mean…it's only us who need to get back on the train after four days.'

'What gave you that idea?' Maud demanded. 'We're doing the whole thing, like you. Adelaide to Darwin. Then we're taking a boat ride from Darwin to Broome. After that…' She looked doubtfully at Hugo and her cheerfulness faded a little. 'After that, Hugo has to make up his mind whether he'll take over the company or go back to Afghanistan. He has some hard thinking to do, and it's lovely that he has some company while he does it.'

How could a man sleep? The bed was too soft. The night was too still—and Amy was right through the wall.

Finally he headed outside, across the home paddock to the spring-fed waterhole beyond.

The waterhole had been dug forty years ago, and now seemed part of the landscape. It was surrounded by natural foliage, a protected place where creatures of the night could come and drink their fill.

He walked stealthily, with the tread of a soldier. The night creatures ignored him and kept on with their business. He headed for a huge flat rock, a place where he could watch over the water and see Uluru with the moon behind it.

He sat and watched, and tried to still his mind. A wallaby was drinking beside him. That was the only company he wanted.

Decisions.

Ruling Thurston Holdings, or returning to Afghanistan?

Taking his place as head of the company his grandfather had founded, or taking refuge in the danger and adrenalin that was his life as a soldier?

He had the knowledge to take over the company. Ever since childhood, his grandfather had talked him through what he was doing with the company he loved. All his life he'd received a weekly letter from his grandfather, outlining what was happening, the repercussions of decisions, the day-to-day minutiae of Thurstons.

For the last twenty years, those letters had been Hugo's link to home, but what he hadn't realised until now was how much they'd taught him of the company, from the inside out.

So all he had to do was say yes. Step into the limelight. Be the Thurston who headed Thurstons.

Did he have a choice? He'd been putting it off, but the alternative was Thurston Holdings becoming just another corporate power. With Thurstons behind him, he could do more good in the world than one man ever could in Afghanistan.

His last tour of duty had been appalling. A roadside bomb. Two of his closest colleagues…

They stayed with him in his dreams, and to go back there…

The alternative meant stepping back into the media spotlight he'd hated as a child. But he could handle it, he thought bleakly. He'd learned a lot about life in his long years in the army. He could handle anything, as long as he was alone.

So tonight…why was a slip of a girl who could pirouette on damp sand messing with his head?

'Because I'm stupid,' he said aloud and the wallaby was startled and leaped away.

'Sorry,' he said as he realised the wallaby wasn't the only creature he'd shocked. 'I need to get a grip.'

By tomorrow. By the next time he saw her.

Four days with Amy?

So why did the prospect have him sitting outside, thinking of her more deeply than the huge changes in his life that lay before him?

Why did the prospect seem as huge and as troubling as his decision to take over Thurstons?

CHAPTER SIX

MAUD was in charge. On her turf she was like a general commanding her troops. Nobody argued.

Hugo knew better than to argue. He sat at breakfast and watched Maud bully Rachel to eat. He watched Amy relax, and he thought these two could both use some grandmotherly support. It'd also take pressure off him if Maud grandmothered them instead of him. Win-win for everyone.

'What are you grinning at?' Maud demanded as she pushed a second coffee at Rachel. Creamy coffee. 'You have work to do. If we don't have the car ready soon it'll be midday and too hot to enjoy it.'

'Yes, ma'am,' he said and went to get the car.

Buster was staying at home. 'Dogs aren't allowed in the Uluru reserve,' Maud said, and Amy wasn't pushing this one. Wendy, the housekeeper, was lovely, and more than happy to care for one small dog. Hugo brought the car to the front door and they were ready.

Amy was carrying her purse. Her big purse.

'You know,' he said thoughtfully, 'Wendy's promised to take excellent care of him. There are good reasons why dogs aren't permitted in the National Park.'

'It's not Buster.'

'Steak sandwich recipes, then?' And then he saw the look on her face and stopped.

Her purse was bulging, but not with dog. Something angular and solid.

He looked at Amy's face and saw tension—and he looked at Rachel and saw the same.

He saw their matching expressions and suddenly he knew.

A grandmother who'd always wanted to come home. A baby.

The way Amy clutched her bag.

They'd come all this way?

'I won't be doing a purse search,' he said gently, and Amy's shoulders sagged, just a little. He thought: she's been carrying this burden for far too long.

He smiled at her and she tried to smile back, but it didn't come off. She cast him a look of gratitude that did something to his insides. Something he'd never felt before.

* * *

Maud chattered happily all the way to Uluru, and he didn't stop her. They all needed Maud's chatter.

Every now and then he glanced in the rear view mirror. Rachel looked pale and tense, and he saw Amy was holding her hand.

His gut twisted at the look on Amy's face.

Soon, he promised her silently. Soon at least one burden will be lifted.

He knew.

How he'd guessed she didn't know, but the way he'd looked at her… It was as if he could read her, she thought, and she wasn't sure whether to like it or reject it out of hand. She should reject it, she thought, but this was Hugo and there was something about Hugo…

Don't go there.

They drove to the base of Uluru. Hugo showed them the walking trail round the base of the rock. He showed them the waterholes, the places they might be private. Then, suddenly, he was suggesting Maud might like to see something new since last time they'd been here, plants he thought would look great in her garden.

Maud and Hugo seemed to melt away, leaving

Amy alone with Rachel—and the contents of her purse.

They walked on.

Uluru.

Their grandmother had talked about this place with such awe, with such love, that Amy had scarcely believed it could be so amazing. She'd thought the magic of the rock must be partly a figment of a child's nostalgic longings. But now, as she and Rachel watched water from recent rain trickle in rivulets down the gigantic rock face, as she laid her hands on the sun-warmed rock, weathered by thousands of years' exposure to the desert winds, she thought no, this place called to her as it had called to Bess.

She glanced at Rachel and saw she was feeling the same.

'I'm glad we came,' Rachel said simply, and then they found the right place and they did what they'd come to do.

For years Bess's ashes had lain in a concrete plinth in a city crematorium. It had never felt right, but now they sat on a sun-warmed rock, and two lots of ashes, one large, one small, were joined and sprinkled into the water. The water here pooled, clear and beautiful, then ran on through the rocks, down into some secret waterway under the earth.

This was right, Amy thought, as the ashes washed underground, under this vast rock, this place Bess had called home.

And when it was done something had cleared from Rachel's face. 'This is right,' she said softly. She looked up at the vast rock face and she sighed. 'What happened can't mess with my life any more. My daughter's here and she's with Grandma, and it's time to let her go.'

She was weeping. Amy turned to give her some privacy and she glimpsed Hugo in the distance—holding Maud back.

He waved, a barely perceptible movement, but his meaning was clear. Take as long as you want. As long as you need.

She closed her eyes in gratitude, for this man, for this place, for now. She'd brought Rachel to the place where Bess had promised they could find peace, and they had. She could move on from this moment.

And somehow, the fact that Hugo knew, the fact that Hugo understood, made it better.

Stupid? Maybe it was, she thought as she hugged

Rachel, but that was the way it was and there was nothing she could do about it.

The native people held this place as sacred and Hugo could understand why. He felt it a little, and he respected it more.

He showed Maud the plants. She appreciated them but she was smart—she knew she was being diverted.

'There's more to this for the girls than just looking at a rock,' she said. 'Do you know what?'

Maud was great, he thought, loving her even more. How many women would be as intuitive as she was?

'They've been through a lot,' he told her, and then he told her as much of Rachel's story as he knew, and what he suspected they were doing now. Amy would agree, he thought, for Maud in healer mode was a power to be reckoned with.

'They're lovely girls,' Maud said when he finished, and then she glanced thoughtfully at Hugo. 'But Amy's special.'

'They're both…okay.'

'They're more than okay,' she declared. 'And you and Amy… You've just told me her secrets—you, the world's best secret-keeper. Amy trusts you, and now you're trusting me as well.' She frowned, thinking it through. 'That means you know Amy won't mind you sharing with me. You *know* Amy.'

'Maud...'

'I'm just saying,' she said speculatively, even mischievously. 'I'm saying Amy *is* special and I'm saying don't mess with it.'

Rachel wilted soon after, and so did Maud. They returned to the house and Maud retired to her bedroom. Rachel swam in the pool, then went to sleep on a sun lounger. Hugo retreated to his grandfather's study to immerse himself in the business of Thurston Holdings.

Trying not to think about Amy?

Work... Thurstons. He already had a handle on this. He could do it. There were challenges he could get his teeth into.

So why did it feel so bleak?

Because he was facing it alone?

He liked being alone, he told himself. Of course he did. When had he not?

There were odd sounds coming from the veranda. He glanced beyond the curtains and Amy was at the veranda rail, steadily working through some sort of practice routine.

She was wearing tights, a T-shirt and bare feet. She was moving through action after action, each movement designed to stretch her body to the limit.

She looked amazing, he thought, and it was all he could do not to fling open the windows and join her.

Only that'd mean she'd stop. No.

He watched her and he wondered. Maud had said she'd been one of Australia's best dancers. What must she be feeling, to walk away?

He watched her, her grace, her beauty, and the suspicion surfaced again that she'd chosen this path. After her sister's accident she'd moved from principal roles to dancing in the background. Now, as her sister needed to move on, suddenly she was retiring for ever?

She'd hinted it was through body fatigue. She'd intimated she hurt as much as Maud did.

She wasn't hurting now. What she was doing was amazing.

Something was twisting within him. Aching.

That something wasn't allowed to ache, he told himself harshly. He had no business wanting… what he was wanting.

The sensations of the morning came flooding back. The tension on Amy's face. The way she'd held Rachel.

Amy.

No. He turned back to his grandfather's desk. To his grandfather's world.

There was a bunch of newspaper cuttings on the side—Wendy must have gathered them for Maud. They were tributes written when James had died, but littered throughout were pictures taken at random, many taken by people like the guy on the train.

Public intrusion. Public exposure.

If he took over Thurstons he could ignore this, he thought. He must. This wasn't a path he'd have chosen to tread, but there'd be satisfaction in getting it right.

And the path Amy was choosing?

Amy's choice was no business of his.

But what if their worlds merged?

He glanced again at the media clippings and his mind closed to the random dumb thought. What was he thinking? He wouldn't put any woman he loved into that sort of goldfish bowl.

Any woman he loved? Where had that come from?

Nowhere, he thought savagely, and that was where it could go. Nowhere.

Go back to work. Maud could matchmake all she liked. It wasn't on.

Maud and Rachel fitted like hand in glove. Rachel was fragile and needed nurturing. Maud needed someone to nurture. She'd been trying to nurture Hugo, but there was only so much nurturing a soldier could take.

The next morning, when Maud started collecting pillows to make the sun loungers more comfortable, he thought of a hundred other things he should be doing.

So did Amy. 'I might take a walk,' she said hastily, but Rachel looked longingly at the pillows.

Maud grinned. 'Exactly. Let me tell you my plans for our day.' As Hugo backed away she caught his arm. 'No, Hugo. Rachel and Buster and I need our beauty sleep, but Rachel's been telling me she needs rock samples from the Olgas. So that's what I've planned.'

'What?' Hugo said cautiously, but he already knew what was coming.

'It's a gorgeous walking day,' Maud decreed. 'I've asked Wendy to prepare a picnic lunch for the two of you. You can take James's old back-pack, carry lunch there and carry rocks home. Rachel, you tell Hugo what rocks you want and he'll bring them home to you.' She beamed from Amy to Hugo and back again. 'You two can walk the whole Olgas today. Ooh, I wish I was young enough to join you.'

She didn't look as if she wished she could join them. She looked like a Machiavellian old…old… Words failed him.

She was oblivious. 'I knew you'd love the idea,' she said happily. 'Off you go and put on suncream and sturdy boots—you have got sturdy boots, Amy? Don't get lost. If you're not back by midnight we'll send out a search party. Oh, and take Amy home via Uluru at sunset, Hugo. Rachel and I will go over in the other car and meet you. You don't mind spending the day with me, do you, Rachel?'

'No,' Rachel said, looking thoughtful, and then rather pleased. 'I'd love to.'

'There you go, then,' Maud said, sounding smug. 'Not an objection in sight. Off you go, the pair of you, and have fun.'

* * *

It was thirty miles to the base of the Olgas. Hugo drove in silence. He was doing what he always did, which was retreating into himself.

Self-protection? Yes, it was, and he wasn't ashamed to admit it. His nightmares were too close—too real—to leave himself unprotected.

Ten minutes. Fifteen. Still silence.

'I know you've been hijacked but do you have to play the martyr?' Amy asked at last, sounding strained.

'Sorry?'

'It's incredibly generous of you and your grandma to have us stay,' she said. 'And it was even more generous of Maud to make you bring me to the Olgas. I know you were bulldozed, but so was I. I didn't want to be under obligation but I can't help it. We're in this together, so if you're going to sulk…'

'I'm not sulking!' he said, astonished.

'No?'

'No! I just like my own company.'

'Well, bully for you. You know this is not my call,' she snapped. 'Rachel wants her rocks. Maud wants you to come with me and I can't get to the Olgas by myself. You're stuck so you might as well be sociable.'

'I'm no good at small talk.'

'You're a man of action,' she said. 'I can see that.' She hesitated. 'Are you hating the thought of taking over from your grandpa?'

'No!'

More silence.

'Okay, then,' she said, determinedly cheerful. 'Next topic?'

'We don't need to talk.'

She looked at him thoughtfully. Really thoughtfully.

'Okay, then,' she said at last, and wriggled down further into the car seat. 'Go right ahead and sulk. I might even join you.'

She wanted small talk.

He glanced across at the determined set of her mouth, the flash of anger in her eyes. The cute way her nose…

No.

Solitude.

Silence.

He was being a bore and she was starting to be angry.

They'd hardly talked by the time they reached the foot of the Olgas. Hugo heaved the lunch/rock pack onto his back and set off. Amy put her own smaller pack on and trudged determinedly by his side. In silence.

She was enjoying herself, she told herself. She must be. In this place, how could she not?

The Olgas were vast domes jammed hard into one another, each dome the size of a small mountain. Walking trails snaked throughout. With Rachel's list to guide them, they set off through the Valley of the Winds, the trail the guidebooks said was the loveliest in the range.

They seemed to have the place to themselves, though the domes were so huge there could be crowds hidden here and they wouldn't know. The breeze meant it wasn't too hot, and the creeks meandering across their path and the fact that they could scoop mountain water over their faces at every ford made it feel even cooler.

Hawks were circling in the thermals above their heads, watching them with idle interest. They looked awesome. It should be the most awesome day, she thought. It was. But what was it with this guy beside her?

'Do you think I'm planning on jumping you?' she asked at last, trying for a reaction—for any reaction.

'Don't be daft,' he said, attempting a smile, but he kept right on striding. She was keeping up easily but she was fit. A lesser woman would have been left behind in the car park.

Maybe that was what he wanted.

'I'm not stupid and I wouldn't jump you if you paid me,' she snapped. 'Hugo, stop now. If you find my company so obnoxious, how about you give me half the lunch, half the list of the rocks Rachel wants and we meet back in the car park when we're done? I know Maud's trying to set us up but that's not my fault and if we separate now your grandma will never know.'

He did stop then.

They were standing on a ridge between two of the great domes. The scenery in both directions was breathtaking. The wind right now was wafting gently through the valley, but the trees were bent and gnarled with the fiercer wind that had given the place its name.

Right now, however, the scenery was immaterial. Hugo had stopped. She needed to think of something to say.

He looked tense. He also looked tough, battle-trained, ready for anything. How hard must it be, she wondered, to come from the world's confrontations to here?

Say nothing—or ask?

When had she ever been the shrinking violet?

'Hugo, what's eating you?' she demanded, and the irritation she'd been feeling all morning boiled over. 'You don't want to be here? Am I the problem, or is it something else? Where else do you want to be? On some battlefield somewhere, or behind your grandpa's desk? Right now you're in what I imagine must be one of the most beautiful places in the whole world—*and you're sulking?*'

'I am not sulking,' he said and turned as if to keep walking.

'You are so sulking,' she yelled after him, and all the frustration, the humiliation of being treated as a duty, the worry about Rachel, her future, everything, all boiled over in that one yell.

Her yell sounded out over the valley and the echo came straight back at her, the valley ringing with the cadence of her fury. And it didn't stop. Over and over it echoed, bouncing off the valley walls. Her anger was everywhere.

Sulking...king...king...king...

Whoa, she thought, stunned, and then, despite

her shock, she felt her lips twitch. She thought: if I'm going to insult a guy, why not do it in style?

How would he react to being so publicly chastised? She could see no one, but that echo would be carrying her voice all the way to Uluru.

And his blank look had faded. He was staring at her as if she had two heads.

She couldn't take it back. The echo of her insult went on and on, as if the mountains themselves were accusing.

Would he explode right back?

She thought about apologising. She decided she was still too angry. And, ridiculously, laughter was too close.

She tried desperately to focus just on her anger. She'd looked forward to being here for so long, yet his grumpiness was spoiling it for her. She'd rather be on a tour group than this.

'You should have let us stay at the resort,' she muttered, trying not to sound defensive.

'You want to yell that down the valley, too?'

He was angry, she thought. *He was angry at her.*

He didn't even get why she might be even mildly irritated and suddenly she was a whole lot more than mildly irritated. She'd thought this guy was empathic, kind, not to mention sexy as hell. Even though she'd assured him she had no intention of jumping him, she'd set off today with a tiny frisson of excitement about spending the day with him. And okay, she conceded. Maybe it wasn't so tiny.

But now… How he was behaving… She met his tense gaze and she decided her tension hadn't exploded enough. She was going to laugh or cry or…what? She had to do something—and this guy deserved everything he was about to get.

She turned and faced down into the valley and she cupped her hands and she yelled.

'You should have let us stay at the res…'

He grabbed her and whirled her to face him, clamping his hand hard on her mouth.

She writhed in fury. He released her mouth but his hands moved to her shoulders as if he was ready to take further action at first yell.

'Oi,' she managed, struggling to haul free. 'Let go of me. You want to take this to the next level?'

'And what would that be?' he demanded, sardonic, and she couldn't resist. His hands were on her shoulders. Of all the great positions…

Do it.

She did.

CHAPTER SEVEN

ONE minute he was holding her hard, stopping her from yelling. The next he was lying on his back, staring at the sky.

He'd been flipped, by a girl almost a foot shorter than him. By a ballet dancer. By the girl his body had been studiously trying to ignore all morning.

He was a commando.

She'd flipped him as if he were a pancake.

She'd backed away. She was watching from a distance, waiting for him to get up, waiting to see if she should run.

If his men could see him now…

He'd thought before how cute her nose was. From this angle…everything was cute.

The way she was looking at him. Apprehension plus.

His anger, his frustration receded. There was only here, only now. His lips twitched.

He really should get up.

It was kind of peaceful lying here. A hawk was

wheeling just above his head. Maybe he could lie here for a while. Take in what had just happened.

Make her worry?

'Have I hurt you?' she asked and there was doubt creeping in. Worry? Indignation was still there, though. In spades.

'Yes,' he said conversationally, 'I believe you have.'

'Hugo...'

Was there fear in her voice?

He'd been flipped in a classic martial arts throw. He'd landed flat on his back as she'd intended. Such a throw, onto flat ground, wouldn't normally do damage, but, of course, she hadn't checked the ground for rocks or other hazards before she'd thrown.

'You've hurt my dignity,' he said, and saw a wash of relief on her face—fast replaced by a response worthy of a warrior.

'Well, as long as I haven't squashed our sandwiches,' she threw back, and he almost choked.

She'd thrown him and she was able to come straight back at him, pretending the flash of fear she knew he'd seen wasn't for him but for her lunch.

She was...amazing.

'The sandwiches are fine,' he admitted. 'I believe they're in a plastic container. I can feel the box digging into my spine.'

'Thank heaven for that. I'd forgotten about lunch.'

'So if you'd remembered, you'd have asked me to take the backpack off first?'

'I'd have brought you down on your side instead.'

He sat up and gazed at her with incredulity. She stared back, still defiant, but also…a little bit scared. Was she afraid he'd retaliate?

Worse, maybe she was afraid he'd go straight back to being the bore that he'd been all morning. Maybe he'd deserved to be thrown.

'Karate?' he asked conversationally.

'Tae Kwon Do.'

'You learn Tae Kwon Do as part of ballet training?'

She relaxed a little. Just a little. 'My grandma always said a woman needs to look after herself,' she said, talking a bit fast. Nerves were still front and centre. 'She sent us to lessons from the age of five. It was through Tae Kwon Do that I discovered ballet—my teacher told me I had natural ability.'

'So you and Rachel both learned?' he said, watching her with a certain amount of caution. 'Can Rachel throw a man, too?'

'Any man you care to mention.'

'And I've invited two of you to stay!'

'We're peaceable,' she said, and he thought she was having trouble sounding peaceable. 'We only defend ourselves—and, unlike some we could mention, we've never carried machine guns.' She lifted her finger, blew imaginary powder from its trigger and reholstered it with a cowboy-like shrug. 'Our bodies are our defence.'

He laughed. He couldn't help himself. No, she wasn't carrying a machine gun. She wasn't a threat. She was, though, quite simply adorable. Yeah, Maud was matchmaking, and no, he couldn't take this further even if he wanted— though there was a big part of him saying that was a shame and a half. But his problems were his problems and to make her day miserable because of them was unforgivable.

So get a grip, he told himself, and he eased the backpack around and flipped it open.

'Truce,' he said. 'Sandwiches?'

She didn't move. She was standing ten feet away and she was still looking cautious.

'They're not loaded,' he said. 'I believe they're egg and lettuce, and roast beef and salad.'

'I shouldn't have thrown you.'

'Not before you made sure the sandwiches were safe. I agree.'

'No retaliatory action?'

'I've retired from action.'

'Really?'

'Really,' he said.

She still didn't come close.

'Is that another way of saying you've retired from the army and life's about to get boring?'

Where had that come from? One minute they were talking about Tae Kwon Do. The next they were talking about his life?

'Like you and ballet, I suspect,' he said, trying to keep it light. 'We're buying ourselves carpet slippers and stoking up our sitting room fires.'

'I can't see you as the head of Thurston Holdings in carpet slippers.'

'I can't see me as head of Thurston Holdings. Have a sandwich.'

She ventured close and squatted beside him— still a wee bit cautious—and chose a sandwich, then settled on a rock nearby and ate half before she said anything more. 'What do you see your-self as?' she asked.

'Private,' he said before he gave himself time to think about it. But she thought about it. She was watching him, considering, weighing him up. She ate a bit more sandwich before she responded.

'I'd imagine,' she said at last, 'that the head of Thurston Holdings can buy private.'

She was probing where she had no place to be. She was pushing into his solitude, but the thought came suddenly: this is Amy. This woman is no threat.

Or not in any way he'd known before.

'I can come here,' he told her. 'That's why James built this place. No one in his face.'

'Scary things, cameras.'

'You can't imagine.'

'You're scared?'

'No.'

'No,' she said thoughtfully. 'But I imagine you're wary. Rumours are your parents liked the media attention, and as a kid that must have been appalling. Is that why you went into the army?'

See, that was the problem with media atten-tion. The whole world knew about his childhood. Including this chameleon of a woman. This woman who made him feel…

No. Do not feel. 'That's…'

'None of my business,' she agreed. 'Can I have another sandwich?'

'Have three.'

'And shut up?'

'You said it.'

'Fine,' she said and subsided.

She really did subside. What was more, she didn't seem to mind subsiding. She was no longer accusing him of sulking; she was simply content to retire into her own space.

She wandered across the ridge as she ate her sandwiches. She munched an apple and drank her water. She checked out the view from every angle. She squatted and watched a bunch of bull ants filing in and out of their nest. She gazed upward at the hawks soaring above them.

Then she lay back on a sun-warmed rock, put her hands behind her head and closed her eyes. She was waiting for him to finish his lunch, or waiting for him to tell her it was time to go, or waiting for him to tell her it was okay, she was allowed to talk again.

She was infuriating. Fascinating.

Irresistible?

'You can talk,' he said at last, goaded. 'I thought we weren't doing the sulking thing any more.'

'Shush.'

'What do you mean, shush?'

'You're messing with my serenity, plus I'm in the middle of a plan.'

'Which would be?' This woman, he thought, seemed to have an infinite capacity to surprise him.

'For how you can cope with the media when you hate it. I've watched your grandpa in action. He was great.'

'They never let him alone.'

'He was too nice,' she said thoughtfully. 'Too polite—except for when he was wild on Maud's account. But anger's not good, either. That gets you more attention. And neither is being good-looking,' she added, obviously thinking as she spoke. 'The problem for your grandpa, of course, was that he had dignity. And Maud was beautiful, so he and Maud were media darlings.' She was surveying him with care. 'But you're good-looking, too, plus you're a soldier. That's infinitely sexy. The women's pages will love you. So I'm thinking... Maybe the best idea is to dye your hair grey—I think a sort of yellowish-grey is best, none of your distinguished white—and start wearing home-knitted pullovers.'

He choked.

'There,' she said approvingly. 'You agree? My plan has you in Fair Isle sweaters—maybe something a yodeller would wear, one of those guys who carries cute little accordions and do tap dances on the side. That's fashion. Then…presentation… I think when anyone asks you anything, you should just bore them to death. Like if they say: why did Thurstons' share price drop this week? You tell them it's the same set of conditions that existed in ninety-four, or was that ninety-three, and before that maybe eighty-one. You drone on a bit about why they varied then. Then you say: have you ever noticed how share prices seem to be as variable as the weather? Like today, the forecast is for great weather, but that weird cloud over there is looking threatening. Maybe the wind will spring up, just like it did last weekend when you were trying to read the papers after your morning coffee. Has anyone else noticed how hard it is to read those wide broadsheets? Are you guys responsible for paper sizing? And, by the way, has anyone noticed how the quality of coffee's gone off in the past few years? Why don't they write a piece on that instead of haranguing you?'

She grinned as he looked stunned. 'Okay, that's detail,' she told him. 'But you need something more—broader brush strokes.' She considered for a bit and then nodded, decision made. 'I know. I think you need a chatty wife who wears tweeds and who has a moustache. I believe she should be interested in something like turnip propagation. You should then have at least six children who are all brainy, who are all passionate about turnips and who don't do drugs except for turnip fertiliser.'

She wrinkled her brow, thinking it through a bit more. 'I suspect that'll work,' she decreed at last. 'Have I missed anything? I agree, it'll take planning but you're a soldier—planning's your thing. That's that. Can we get on with our day now?'

'I guess we can,' he said a trifle unsteadily.

'Excellent,' she said and hauled Rachel's list out of her pocket. 'The dome to the left of us looks like our first destination. Rachel wants a core sample chipped two inches in, taken just below the summit. She has GPS coordinates here. You want to chip or shall I?' She'd been carrying a light pack. She swung it round, hauled it open and produced a sharp-looking pick.

'You told me you weren't armed,' he said, trying—and failing—to keep his voice steady. 'Maybe I'm not brave enough to accompany you.'

'That's fine,' she said and started packing up the sandwiches. 'I'm good on my own. I promised I'm not about to jump you. Neither shall I use my pick or my martial arts, but if you want to split up, I'm happy.'

'I won't be,' he said and pulled himself together and hauled his backpack back on. Trying not to laugh. Trying to focus on something other than Amy.

Rachel's list.

The Olgas.

It was no good. Amy was front and centre. She was simply…gorgeous.

They worked steadily for two hours, climbing from site to site, taking the samples Rachel had asked for, taking notes, taking pictures from every angle of the sites where they'd removed the rock—taking pleasure in each other's company.

The talk was still pared to a minimum but things

had changed. He'd relaxed and so had Amy. She was enjoying herself, he thought, and so was he.

The work was physically hard. Rachel had suggested they take two days to do it, or even not finish—she'd listed her samples in order of importance so if they didn't finish it was no drama—but there was no thought of stopping.

They were blessed by the weather. They had plenty of drinking water and sunscreen. There were shady spots to stop for breaks but Amy didn't need a break.

She rock-hopped like one of the shy wallabies they glimpsed from time to time, and more than once he remembered her decision to retire and thought surely it hadn't been because of physical disability.

He'd trained in some of the harshest conditions in the world, yet she kept up with him with ease. Her hair was tousled by the light wind. Her nose was painted white with sunscreen. She finished taking each sample and looked at the next GPS coordinate with anticipation.

'So why did you retire from the ballet?' he asked once as she leaped a rock chasm that he'd assumed she'd climb around.

'Ooh, I can feel a very long discussion about

wide newspapers and standards of today's coffee coming on,' she said and grinned to take the
sting out of the snub.

He grinned back.

He was loving this.

Loving…*her*?

Um…not. He'd known her a few days. You
didn't fall in love in a few days, and he didn't fall
in love at all.

And she wasn't wearing tweeds and a moustache.

But still… He watched her clambering up a peb-
ble strewn scree, as nimble as a small mountain
goat, and he wondered.

She turned and stared down at him. He was at
the bottom of the scree, just watching her.

'What?' she demanded. And then, 'Would you
like a hand up?'

'No,' he said, revolted.

'Or a wee nap?'

'Amy…'

'Just asking,' she said blithely and turned to continue to climb. 'I'm thinking the Australian army
needs to send their soldiers to our ballet academy
for a bit of toughening up.'

Not so much. He could overtake her in a heartbeat, he thought.

Why would he want to?

'Hugo?'

She'd reached the top of the rise and was standing still, looking away from him. Her voice was suddenly unsure. Worried?

He was with her in seconds, scrambling up the scree as if it didn't exist. 'What's wrong?'

'There's a wallaby.'

There was, not fifteen feet from where she stood.

It wasn't moving.

Was it injured?

She put a hand out to stop him going further, but he knew not to frighten.

The rock wallabies were beautiful, tiny, delicate, kangaroo-like creatures which bounded around this rocky habitat with an ease that was breathtaking. They were also intractably shy. He'd seen glimpses of them during the day, but glimpses only. In daylight hours they'd be hiding in the shadows. Hugo had felt watched every moment they'd been here, and these creatures were the reason why.

A shadow passed over their heads—a great

wheeling hawk—and he saw the wallaby cringe but not move.

The hawk was in surveillance mode. Exposed on the rock ledge, the wallaby was an easy target. The hawk was wheeling, watching, waiting to move in for the kill. If he and Amy hadn't arrived, the wallaby might already be taken.

'Why is she here?' Amy breathed. 'She must be injured.'

In which case, maybe it was kinder to simply back off and let the hawk get on with it, Hugo thought grimly. It'd be a swift end.

'Amy…'

'I know,' she whispered, desolate. 'I'm my grandma's daughter and I know bush ways. I'm not suggesting we take an old, ill wallaby and pay a fortune on vet's bills and then try and rehabilitate it when the end's inevitable. But…'

But. Both of them were thinking but.

'Her pouch is extended,' Hugo said after a while. 'But empty.'

They watched on. Above them, the hawk looped lazily, content to wait until they moved away before it did what had to be done.

What was wrong with it?

Hugo knew rock wallabies. He knew joeys

stayed with their mother until they were almost fully mature. By the time they were half-grown the mother's pouch was starting to look stretched and saggy.

As was this one. The pouch was sagging, but there was no bulge inside. There was no joey in sight.

Maybe the hawk had taken it?

If it had, he thought, why was the wallaby staying here, in full sun, when the hawk was still wheeling overhead? When their presence must be pushing her every instinct to flee.

There was a ledge right beside her.

'Let's see,' he said, and inched forward, trying not to startle the animal more than he must.

He got to within about ten feet of the wallaby before she moved, which in itself was astonishing. It made him think she must be hurt, but when she finally bounded away there was no trace of injury. She took three fast leaps into the shadows of the rock-face behind, but then she stopped. She was still not far enough to make him think this was a normal retreat.

He'd reached the ledge. He looked down, and by the time he did he almost expected what he saw.

Here was her joey, gangly and half-grown.

Stuck.

The ledge formed the side of a crevice almost fifteen feet deep. Smooth red rock rose on every side, almost vertical. The crevice was too high to jump out of, too steep to climb.

At the base was flat ground, sandy, smooth. Littered with bones.

This was a trap for the unwary, he thought, seeing exactly how it could happen. An immature joey, filled with youthful confidence, that his mother could keep him safe from danger, had bounded too close and slipped.

He mustn't have been there for long. He looked alert, sitting back on his haunches, looking upward. His head was cocked on one side, as if he were asking: Mum, what's taking you so long to get me out?

There was no way his mother could get him out, and if she stayed peering down at him she'd be the hawk's next meal.

'Oh, no.' Amy had slid up to lie beside him. 'How can we get him out?'

Signs in the car park were clear as to how tourists were to handle wildlife. Short answer—don't. This was a National Park. Nature could seem harsh, but if humans interfered then the balance was upset. The hawk had to eat.

Maybe, Hugo thought, but leaving a wallaby facing a quick death from a hawk was a far cry from knowing that its mother's death meant slow dehydration for the joey below.

But how to get down there? Fifteen feet…

'You didn't bring a ladder in your backpack, I suppose?' Amy asked.

'No.' He was trying to think. He had no rope. The sides were too steep to get down and up again.

He could radio the rangers and ask them to help, he thought, but the signs back in the car park made him pause. He knew what their answer would be.

But to walk away…

Maybe he could make a rope, but there was nothing to tie it to. He searched the vertical walls for toe holds and found none.

'If we made a rope, do you reckon you could hold me?' Amy asked.

'Hold you?'

'Lower me down and up again. I'm not all that heavy. My partners heave me round all the time. I know ballerinas have better training regimes than soldiers, but if you tried very hard…'

He had to smile. But… 'You're not going down,' he said. 'What if you got stuck?'

'Then you'll lower the rest of the sandwiches and the water and go for help. I'll play the dumb tourist and there'll be rescue helicopters here in no time.'

'To pull you out of a chasm.'

'With Joey,' she said. 'If I can hide Buster, I can hide him—though a helicopter would probably make his mother take fright. It'll be better if you can just grit your teeth and pull.'

'Pull what?' He was already devising ways and means but he wanted to see what she'd come up with.

'Do you have a knife, soldier boy?'

'Yes.' Of course he did. A knife that did everything.

'Job done,' she said in satisfaction. 'I'd volunteer my trousers but there's my dignity to consider—and there's also no need. We have backpacks. We slice strips and knot.'

'Did they teach rope-making in ballet school?' he demanded, astounded.

She giggled. 'Buster training,' she said. 'Our foster parents said he had to sleep outside and our bedroom was upstairs. Knotting sheets is harder than you think, so we chopped Rachel's hold all. We tied knots every eighteen inches and it made an awesome ladder. What are we waiting for?'

What indeed?

Nothing, except that he needed to look at her—just look—before he took her backpack and started slicing.

Hugo was far better at rope-making than she was, Amy admitted. And faster. He stripped out the lining. He cut the toughened outer fabric into strips. He tested each strip for strength, then knotted them together with knots that were truly impressive. No granny knots for Hugo Thurston. This guy was a commando and it showed.

She glanced over to the mother wallaby.

'Don't be afraid,' she told her. 'The cavalry's here in the shape of the Australian Armed Forces.'

'The Australian Armed Forces don't go much for lowering ballerinas into crevices to pull out wallabies,' Hugo retorted.

'Then their training's lacking.' She tugged at the rope. 'This is really strong. I can't slide, though.'

'You won't slide. You'll belay yourself down like a climber. You loop your wrist round like this and hold, then do the same with your next wrist. Use the knots. Take some of your weight onto your feet before you change wrists.'

'Like a professional.'

He gave a grim smile. 'Right. We do this professionally or not at all. When you get down, use my backpack for the joey. Zip him up and tie him to our rope. I'll bring him up before you.'

'See,' she said admiringly, speaking to the mother wallaby again. 'I bet he's good at war games, too.'

'And you'll use my shirt,' he said, tugging it off and tossing it to the bottom of the crevice. 'Don't try and catch him with your bare hands. Cover him and bundle him into the pack before he knows what's hit him.'

She could. This was an excellent plan.

So if it was an excellent plan, why was she suddenly breathless?

Because Hugo Thurston had taken off his shirt. *Because Hugo Thurston was naked from the waist up.*

She'd seen men's bodies before. Of course she had. She'd had boyfriends, and she'd danced with near-naked men.

None like this.

For Hugh Thurston did not have a ballet dancer's body. This man was pure warrior. He was toned for hard living, every muscle built for a purpose. He was lean and brown and sinewy, hard and…ripped.

It was a body to take a woman's breath away.

There was a scar running from his left armpit around and under his ribs. It was pale against his tan. The compulsion to touch it was almost irresistible.

She couldn't resist. She reached out, feeling the strength of his body, feeling the faint jerk of a reaction as her skin touched his.

'Hugo…' she breathed and he caught her hand. 'I…I'm sorry. But…what happened?'

'It's my warrior wound,' he said and grinned. 'Every warrior has one.'

'Wh…what?' She was totally disconcerted. She had no business to be asking. She had no business to be touching.

He had no business to be grinning—but he was.

'You want the truth? I fell off my scooter when I was eight, and I was carrying a drink bottle. But if you knew the stories I've told—how much it adds to my street cred…'

He was still smiling. She wanted to smile back,

but her eyes were still caught by his. He was still holding her hand.

He was so close…

'A warrior,' he said softly, still smiling, 'does not allow himself to be deflected from his duty by reminiscing about past wounds. We have a wallaby to save. You want a drum roll before we send you into battle?'

And somehow, finally, she managed to smile back.

'Don't drop me,' she managed.

'I won't let you go,' he said and she felt something jolt inside her.

He was talking about the rope. He was talking about what was happening now.

But suddenly, urgently, and really, really stupidly, she wanted him to be talking about a whole lot more.

Lowering Amy down the crevice was simple. Amy was nimble and strong—and light enough for Hugo to hold her easily.

She didn't mess around. She was down the crevice in seconds.

The joey backed to the furthermost point and trembled.

'You can't stay here,' she told him. 'Look at the bones down here. Ugh.'

Hugo had pulled the rope back up. He attached his backpack and lowered it.

She set it up, open mouthed. All she had to do was catch the joey and pop him in. Easier said than done. The base of the crevice was maybe twenty feet long, eight feet wide.

When Hugo planned this he'd assumed the joey would be weak, maybe even injured, surely shocked to stillness by his ordeal. But this was no shrinking joey. As Amy approached, he leaped high and fast, so high he landed behind her.

Amy whirled and swore.

Uh oh. This was no easy task, Hugo thought. Catching a wild creature…

For the first time, he thought they might not succeed.

But Amy hadn't hesitated. The joey was right at the end of the crevice. Amy carried the shirt towards it slowly, slowly, then, just as he thought the joey would leap again, she crouched and stilled.

'Amy…'

'Hush,' she said. 'We have all the time in the world.'

He hushed.

Amy didn't move. She was totally focused.

His shirt was in her hands and slowly, slowly she extended her hands so the shirt was stretched full like a flag.

Every time the joey twitched, she stopped.

The shirt was out full. She waited.

She waited.

The joey inched forward a tiny bit, imperceptibly moving away from the rock wall, as if readying for another jump.

But Amy jumped first. Her body was like a spring. She flew through the air and the shirt was bundled over the joey before he knew what hit him. He was wrapped and inside the backpack and secure before Hugo even figured what she'd done. She looped the rope through the backpack handles and stood back. Grinning up at him.

'What's keeping you?' she asked.

What, indeed? It had been some sort of ballet move or Tae Kwon Do or something. He'd never seen such a jump.

She was waiting for him to raise one joey. Holding the backpack steady.

He hauled the backpack up, then let the rope down again. 'Your turn,' he told her. 'Put your foot in the loop and I'll pull.'

'Let the joey go first. He needs his mother.'

'Not until you're back up. You need to see this reunion. Besides, with two of us here, the hawk up there's less likely to swoop.' The hawk was hardly likely to swoop just with Hugo, but he wasn't saying that. After such a move, Amy deserved to see mother and baby reunited.

'Let the rope down again, then,' Amy said, sounding exasperated. 'Don't forget Rachel's list. We have important stuff to be getting on with.'

He laughed. He lowered the rope and she stepped into the loop and hung on. 'Are you sure you can you pull?' she asked, sounding dubious. 'I'm heavier than I look.'

He snorted and pulled.

He tugged her up until she caught the edges of the ledge. Then he caught both her hands, tugging her over, making her safe.

The temptation to keep on holding was almost irresistible, but this wasn't the time. Once she was steady, she headed straight for the bulging backpack.

'Take him closer to his mum, into the shade,' he urged.

The adult wallaby had hardly moved. She let

Amy come to within a few feet, backing a little, but not much.

Hugo held back. Amy had done the work. He was more than content to watch.

She unzipped the top. The joey's head came out as if it was peering from a pouch. He peered at Amy, and then he swivelled, searching for what he needed most.

He saw his mother and in one frantic scramble and one huge bound he reached her.

Seconds later he was in his mother's pouch, and mother and baby were melting further into the shadows, where the wind-stunted trees gave cover, where no hawk could see, much less find and swoop.

They were safe.

Home.

'You'd think,' Amy said cautiously, blinking—blinking really hard in fact—'they could have said thank you.'

'I think we can take it as read.' He strolled over and squatted beside her on the ground. 'Well done, you.'

'It was your knots,' she said and blinked even harder.

How was a man to cope with a blinking ballerina?

How could a man not?

He touched her cheek and she turned to him. She was trying very hard to smile. She was trying very hard not to cry.

'We've done our hawk out of his dinner,' she managed and he grinned.

'We'll leave him a beef sandwich. Or do you think he'd like egg and lettuce?'

'Oh, Hugo,' she said and her voice broke. 'Oh, it's magic. This place… Grandma always said it was magic and it is. I wish Rachel could see what we've just done.'

For answer he tugged his phone from his pocket and flipped it open. Here were photos of the joey. Photos of a girl making a flying leap with shirt in outstretched hands. Photos of a joey scrambling into his mother's pouch.

'Your wish is my command, my lady,' he said. 'It's not just creepy guys on trains who carry cameras. The paparazzi have nothing on me.'

'Oh, Hugo,' she breathed, and she smiled and smiled, and it was too much. Smiling through tears had to be his very favourite emotion. Or it was now. Actually, he'd never thought of it until now, but now it definitely was.

And what to do with this very new, very favourite emotion?

He did what any sane man would do in this position.

He put down his phone. He cupped her face in his hands—and he kissed her.

He'd kissed her before, to fluster her, to give her a reason for hiding in his cabin, for purely practical reasons.

That kiss hadn't turned out practical. It had turned out hot. And now, when he kissed for kissing's sake, because he really wanted to kiss her, because she was adorable and smart and cute and irresistible, the heat was turned up a thousandfold.

Maybe the heat had been there all day, simmering, steaming, coming to the boil.

Maybe now…

Maybe what the heck. He was kissing her and it felt as if his brain was fusing.

She felt amazing. She felt…as if she was a part of him. His woman.

What sort of thought was that? He knew. It was

a thought as primeval as time itself, as basic and as needy.

He wanted her and he wanted her now.

He had her. She was melting into his arms. Her mouth was opening to welcome his. Her arms were wrapping themselves around him to hold him tight.

She wanted him as much as he wanted her?

All his life, Hugo Thurston had stayed aloof. His parents' emotional dramas had overplayed his right from the start. How could a five-year-old have a tantrum when his mother had louder ones? He'd learned early that his emotions were irrelevant. He'd learned to hate the tears, the screaming, even the over-the-top excitement and joy that turned the other way without warning. He'd joined the army and thought he'd never succumb.

Enter one slip of a dancer and he'd succumbed.

There'd been women in his life; of course there had. He'd played fair with them, been honest, enjoyed them—and he'd never let them close.

The women he'd dated were the same breed. They'd used him for companionship or immediate need. He'd enjoyed kissing them.

He'd never felt a kiss like this.

If he hadn't known the heat of battle, he might

have thought this was adrenalin, victory from saving the joey, but he'd been in far more adrenalin-filled situations than this.

If he hadn't dated beautiful women he would have said it was desire, but he had.

No. Quit it with the analysis. What he had, right here, right now, was something he'd never experienced and might never experience again.

He was kissing Amy Cotton, and he was loving it.

He felt like a kid kissing for the first time. This first brush of lips, this fierce realisation that here was a whole world of which he knew nothing, this sudden blast of pure, white heat.

This tenderness…

That's what caught him. The fact that he held her in his arms, his mouth claimed hers, the heat was there, but this wasn't a fierce, adrenalin-fed, winner-take-all type of kiss. This was the sweetest of discoveries, the sensation that the woman in his arms was something, someone, who he'd never known existed; had never known could exist.

Her arms were holding him fast. She was kissing him with a fierceness that matched his, but with a tenderness, too, and it was as if he was being bestowed a gift without price.

What price a gift from Amy? How could a woman like this be wanting him?

Stop asking questions. Just savour. Savour the softness of her mouth. Savour the way her breasts moulded to his chest. Savour the way her body clung, curved, folded into his as if she was truly home.

To hold such a woman…

Could he hold such a woman?

If he held her, he'd hurt her. Of course he would; how could he not? A woman as soft as this, as luscious, as lovely—his world would take her and destroy her and spit out what remained.

Shut up, he told himself fiercely. Don't think it now. Just let yourself feel.

For this moment forget you're a soldier. Forget you're a Thurston. You're loving Amy Cotton and nothing else matters in the world.

And Amy… Maybe if he had his shirt on she might retain some level of control, but why would she want to? Hugo's kiss was blasting her into a dimension she hadn't known existed. Her body no longer belonged to her. Her mind no longer belonged to her. She felt herself fold into him, melt into him, and her brain was dissolving into a white hot mist.

Hugo…

It was the one word she could form in her over-heating brain, and even then she couldn't say it. She could only think it, over and over, like a man-tra, as she clung, as she kissed, as she responded to the raw, aching need she felt surge from this man.

He needed her. This was no primitive response to a situation where man and woman were thrown together—or maybe it was, but it was far, far more.

She'd watched his wariness, the way he stood apart from the moment they'd met him on the train, his whole being declaring he was a man who worked in isolation. But right here, right now, there was no isolation at all. She could make love to him right here, she thought, and a part of her exulted in the thought.

It would be her power driving what happened.

Her need?

Was she crazy?

If only he had his shirt on. His mouth was driv-ing her wild but her hands were holding him and the heat, the strength, the feel of his naked skin was driving her wild. She wanted to be closer. Closer...

Things were spiralling, spiralling...

If this man wanted her...

His mouth broke from hers, and she heard herself murmur his name. 'Hugo...'

It came out a plea.

'We can't...' he whispered but his voice was ragged with desire and they both knew they could.

Or maybe... maybe they couldn't.

'Did you see the hawk? Do these things attack humans?'

Company. They'd been alone all day but suddenly they weren't.

Hugo stilled and looked outward, and Amy could have wept in frustration. They were in the shadows, well hidden, but outside a group of tourists was clambering up the scree.

'Hey, the view here's amazing. Honey, you gotta see this... Oh, my...' The voice turned to disgust. 'Someone's left their garbage here. Of all the sacrilegious... We should report it to the rangers. These guys should be shot.'

'It looks like someone's been chopping up a backpack.' The unknown Honey sounded doubtful. 'Look, there's a rope. Maybe someone fell. Just check there's no one down there.'

Silence while the crevice was checked.

'No one,' Honey decreed at last, sounding a tad disappointed. 'But someone should report it to the ranger anyway. They ought to board pits like this up. Anything could happen.'

Anything just had happened, Amy thought. Anything?

'I'll talk to the rangers,' Hugo murmured into her hair as Honey and her party moved on. He was still holding her, but loosely. They both knew the moment was over, that contact needed to cease, but making the final move was hard.

Do not cling to this man.

She stepped back and his hands fell free. She felt...desolate.

'Why will you talk to the rangers?' How much effort did it cost to make her voice sound normal?

'Honey's talking about a pit cover,' he told her. 'This place is beautiful for fences and boarding, but who's to say a tree can't blow over and wedge in the crevice? A rough tree trunk would provide any trapped animal a way to get out. I could organise men to do it.'

'You?'

'We have a mine south of here. I can get a team in here tomorrow.'

But…this wasn't only about making the crevice safe, she thought, watching his face. It was a warning. He wasn't sure where to take this. Neither was she, but he was collecting himself faster. He was reminding himself—and he was reminding her—that he was a Thurston.

This was not a lover to be taken lightly.

A lover? What was she thinking?

Maybe she should do some sharp remembering of why she was here. This holiday was all about Rachel. It had to be. So…

'Thank you for the kiss,' she said as evenly, as resolutely as she could. 'It was…a good way to vent emotions. But we need to get on. Rachel wants rocks.'

'So she does,' he said. His face was wary.

'We're now operating on one pack. That means you get to carry everything.'

'I can do that.'

'Okay, then,' she said, and deliberately turned away. 'I guess you're right,' she said harshly into the stillness. 'Carrying a load alone is what we're both good at. Maybe we need to get on with it.'

CHAPTER EIGHT

THEY worked on methodically and quietly, hardly speaking, collecting every rock sample Rachel had listed, but this wasn't the silence of the morning. It wasn't the silence of a man trapped and a woman angry. This was the silence of two people who knew something momentous had happened and who didn't know where to take it.

If Amy could, she'd have headed for solitude, where she could give her addled mind time to sort itself out. It needed sorting. She felt as if she'd been hit by an electric charge, fused and then re-wired.

She was so aware of Hugo that her mind couldn't get past him. It was lucky Rachel's instructions were simple. Just do the job, she told herself.

Do not think about Hugo.

Who was she kidding? Her head wasn't co-operating. Her head was still filled with sensations she had no hope of controlling. Her body was still filled with the feel of him.

The strength of this man as he'd hauled her from the crevice... The way he'd caught her and held... The look on his face as he'd watched the joey reunited with its mother...

He was a warrior with heart. He was...

Enough! At least he'd put his shirt back on, she thought desperately. A woman would have no hope with it off.

A woman had little hope as it was.

She was holding the bag open while he put samples inside. Their fingers touched and there it was again, a jolt of pure longing.

And he felt it, too. He didn't have to say. It was in his silence, the way he jerked away when his hands touched hers, the way he kept...not looking at her. This was a two-way deal. Whatever she was feeling, he was feeling, too.

Finally, thankfully, they headed back to the car. They should talk all the way down the valley, she thought. There was so much to wonder at in this magnificent place. So much to talk about?

Instead, they walked side by side and things were left unsaid.

But not unthought. Great big thought bubbles

hovered above her head, heavy and grey and so huge she thought Hugo surely must see them.

If he did, he was making no comment.

'It's almost time,' he said brusquely as they reached the car. 'If we hurry we can reach Uluru before sunset.'

Of course. They'd agreed to meet Maud and Rachel. How could she have forgotten?

Hugo had remembered. Maybe he was feeling this…thing…less than she was. Maybe it was just a boy thing—kiss a girl and move on.

There was another bubble to join the warring mob. She climbed into the car, retreated back into silence and let the bubbles fight it out.

The bubbles were finally pretty much coming down on the side of sense.

Even if he was…feeling something, she decided, this guy was a Thurston. She was an ex-ballet dancer, born of a single mum, devoted to her sister and her dog, and even her dog was a mutt. This man was so far out of her league she might as well aim for…

Well, she wasn't aiming. She needed to get to Darwin, start her new job, get Rachel settled and get her life back to normal.

Why didn't he say something?

Concentrate on the landscape, she told herself harshly. Surely that shouldn't be hard.

The sun was sinking low in the sky and the horizon was tinged with gold and fire. Across the barren desert, Uluru glowed like a coal taken from a vast hot furnace. What was it that Rachel said caused it?

'Pink feldspar crystals.' She said it out loud, searching to get practicality into the here and now. This place was making her feel bewitched. This man was making her feel bewitched. 'There's no such thing as magic,' she added and maybe she sounded desperate.

'Ah, but what put the feldspar there?' Hugo said. 'That's what's magic.'

'You should know. You're the mining magnate.'

'My grandpa was the mining magnate.'

'And you're not taking after him?'

'I guess.' The forbidding look descended again.

'There you go, then.' She hugged her knees and glowered, because suddenly she felt like glowering. 'Rachel would have been better as your walking companion today than me. She knows all about rocks. She'd be a better fit.'

'I don't think I need a good…fit,' he said and she flushed.

'Of course not. Sorry.'

'What happened back there...'

'That was silly as well,' she said, talking too fast. 'I'm sorry for that as well.'

'I'm not sorry.'

How to answer that?

She couldn't.

'What will you do in Darwin?' he asked. He was being polite, she thought. Moving on. Good idea. She should, too.

'I'll teach.'

'Dancing?'

'Movement. Including dancing.'

'Who to?'

'Teenagers.' She stared ahead, uncomfortable at the personal interest, but suddenly the glow of Uluru was enough to put discomfort aside. 'Oh...'

For suddenly, thankfully, personal stuff had to be put aside. What lay ahead was enough to make anyone gasp.

The rock was so big that it dwarfed the landscape. As the sun sank, the rock glowed almost as if it was the sun itself. Its colours changed with the changes in the sky, growing brighter by the minute.

There was a car park off the road where a few

people had gathered to watch. Hugo pulled into it and Rachel and Maud bounced forward to meet them.

'We thought you'd miss it.' Rachel caught her sister's hand and practically dragged her forward. 'Come and watch. Oh, Amy…'

Hugo was left with Maud.

They'd both seen Uluru sunsets before. Maud's attention was not on the rock. It was all on Hugo.

'Your shirt's ripped,' she said by way of greeting and he thought: here we go.

He glanced down and his shirt was definitely ripped. One of the joey's claws had caught it.

'By a wallaby,' he said.

'You're looking…'

'Leave it, Grandma.' He turned deliberately away to watch the sunset. Or he turned to watch two women watch the sunset.

Or one woman.

'She's lovely, isn't she?' Maud ventured. 'I know you think she's lovely.'

'She doesn't fit in our world,' he said savagely. 'We'd destroy her.'

Maud stilled. Stood back. Surveyed him again with care.

'You're thinking…' she breathed.

'I can't think. You know the goldfish bowl you've lived in. That's why I left. I hate it. To drag a woman into it... She'd end up like...'

'Your mother?' Maud turned angry, just like that. 'Give Amy some credit. It was the lifestyle that destroyed your parents. It was their own choice.'

'I don't want any part of it.'

'But you will take over Thurstons?'

And suddenly the subject had changed. Matchmaking had become something else. This was something even more important to Maud than Hugo's love life.

Decision time. It had to come, he thought grimly. Would he take over Thurstons?

It was his decision—to stand back and let Thurstons become just another corporate giant, or to keep it as James and Maud had dreamed it should be. An empire with heart. At seventeen he'd run from this decision, but the time for running was past.

He glanced once more at Amy and the thought was heavy. If I take this path...

What other path was there?

No other path was possible.

'Yes,' he said, heavy with the weight of it. 'I will.'

Maud's face sagged with relief. 'Your grandfather would be so proud,' she whispered and hugged him. He held her and he thought: yes, he would.

His grandfather had asked the same of his father, that he take over the responsibility for thousands of employees, for sums of money so staggering he couldn't yet get his head around them.

The responsibility and the media pressure had destroyed his father.

Maybe his character had been weak. Maybe he'd made a bad choice for a wife, but the brutal truth remained. Money and media attention had destroyed him and his wife, and it had come close to destroying Hugo in the process.

For him to survive…

'I'll do it alone,' he said, and his grandmother looked up at him in dismay.

'That makes it sound horrid,' she whispered. 'Like you're entering prison.'

He caught himself. It wasn't for Maud to know just how much he hated this.

'I'm not,' he said and managed a grin. 'They say money and power are like drugs. Any minute now I'll turn into a power-hungry tycoon. Bring on the Armani.'

'You never would,' she said, relaxing again in his laughter. 'You're my Hugo and you'll never change. Hugo, the solitude thing—it's time for it to stop. Amy...'

'No,' he said, and he stopped trying to smile. 'Enough. I'm taking over the company. You've won that battle. Don't try me too far.'

'But you need a nice girl.'

'They threw out the mould when they made you,' he said. 'You've stood up to media attention, scandal, heartbreak, and it hasn't destroyed you. I wish there were two Mauds in the world but there aren't. So leave off the matchmaking. Let me run your company in peace.'

The sun sank further. The rock blazed for one final moment—and then the sun was gone and Uluru was a great grey ghost, settling into the barren landscape to wait for dawn to bring it to life again.

Amy turned and was caught by the sight of a couple a little apart from them. The guy was on bended knee, holding a tiny box towards his lady.

She watched as the girl tugged him up, gathered

him into her arms and they clung. A little bunch of watchers burst into spontaneous applause.

'How lovely,' Rachel said, her eyes misting. 'How perfect.' And the look on her face…

'Rachel…'

'It's okay,' Rachel said softly. 'Just because it didn't work for me doesn't mean I can't be happy for others. Speaking of which… You and Hugo. Spill.'

'Spill what?'

'You're looking…' she surveyed her sister with care '…lit from within. He kissed you?'

'No!'

'He did,' Rachel said jubilantly. 'You're the world's worst liar.'

'So what, then?' Amy said, trying hard not to sound breathless. 'It doesn't mean…' She stopped. 'No,' she said. 'It definitely doesn't mean. I'm on this holiday with you, not with Hugo Thurston.'

'But this is nuts,' Rachel said. 'Hugo's not like Ramón, you know that. He's gorgeous, he's rich, but what's most important is that he's lovely. Maud says he's barely left her since his grandpa died. He hides dogs for complete strangers. He donates steak. How kind was that? Ames, if I met someone like Hugo, would you tell me to be a martyr

and give him up so I could make my sister happy
for another couple of days?'

'Rache…'

'Use your head,' Rachel said. 'And your heart.
That's all I'm saying.'

'You're talking nonsense,' Amy managed. 'A
Thurston and me? In your dreams. I'm sticking
with you, and why wouldn't I? You're prettier,
you're my sister and you're a whole lot safer.'

'Safe's good,' Rachel agreed. 'But…'

'No buts. We have our future mapped. Let's not
mess it with distractions.'

'Hugo Thurston is more than a distraction.'

'No,' Amy said. 'He isn't.'

Dinner was hard. Maud chatted and Amy tried to
join in. Not very successfully. Hugo was too big,
too silent, too *there*. Rachel faded soon after and
excused herself, and Amy did, too.

'I'm achy after today's climb,' she told them,
and Hugo emerged from his silence.

'That's right. I'd forgotten you'd retired from
dancing because your body's wearing out.'

'It happens to us all,' she said, striving for light-
ness. 'Good…goodnight.'

'I won't be here tomorrow,' he said.

She fought to keep her face calm, and somehow she responded as if it didn't matter. It mattered.

'That's…that's fine. Rachel and I are happy just being here. Or we could go back to the resort.'

'You're staying on with me,' Maud growled. 'Hugo's simply decided to take on some of his grandfather's commitments. The company chopper's taking him south to the mines.'

'Was that planned?' Rachel asked Hugo, showing more interest than she'd shown for the whole meal. 'I thought you and Amy…'

Cut it out, Rachel, Amy thought furiously. Why start talking now?

She couldn't say it out loud, but she glared.

Rachel was oblivious. She was waiting for an answer.

'Maybe Amy could go with you,' Maud ventured. 'I'm sure she'd be interested.'

'No.' Hugo and Amy spoke together, and their responses almost matched in their vehemence.

'It was just an idea,' Maud said, placating. 'I know Rachel needs to rest, but I thought Amy…'

'I need to rest, too,' Amy said.

'Because your body's wearing out,' Hugo said dryly.

'Will you cut it out?' She glared and he smiled.

'Sorry. Insensitive of me, I know. But worn out body or not, you don't want to come to the mines. It'd give all sorts of people the wrong idea. Take care of Maud for me.'

'I don't need taking care of,' Maud snapped and Hugo grinned.

'Take care of each other, then, all you achy people. I'm leaving before dawn. I'm not sure when I'll be back, but definitely in time to drive us all back to the *Ghan*.'

'Travel safely,' Amy muttered, and Rachel started to say something, too, but Amy had had enough of this conversation. *The wrong idea?* That had been meant to put her in her place.

This wasn't her place and she knew it. She practically shoved her sister out of the room.

Rachel relaxed. She enjoyed a little sightseeing but mostly she sat on the veranda and sorted the rock samples Hugo and Amy had brought her. She talked to Maud. Maud happily read, swam, snoozed—and talked back. Buster roamed the grounds, lolled in the sun and decided this was pretty much dog heaven.

Amy, on the other hand, paced.

There were things to do. No matter how off balance she was feeling, she intended to make the most of her time here.

She helped Rachel with her rocks. She drove back to Uluru and did the long walk all the way round. She swam. She played with Buster.

She couldn't relax. Inside, she kept right on pacing.

What was wrong with her?

Maud and Hugo had given her the best place to stay a girl could imagine. Rachel was happy, which was the whole aim of this journey. Why wouldn't her mind keep still?

Because her mind was miles away, with Hugo. With the man who'd kissed her senseless.

If he kissed her again...

He wouldn't. He wasn't coming back until it was time to return to Alice Springs. After that, she'd see him only in the corporate and society pages of the media.

How would that feel?

It'll feel like you've been a stupid adolescent with a stupid crush, she told herself. Get over it.

And stop pacing.

'What are you doing after you reach Darwin?' Maud asked, the day before they were due to leave, and it was Rachel who replied. She was happy in Maud's company now, relaxed and amazingly cheerful.

'We both have teaching jobs.'

'Do you start straight away? If not…Hugo and I are taking a cruise. Why don't you come with us?'

The Rachel of two days ago wouldn't have answered. Instead, she looked interested.

'Where are you going?'

'From Darwin to Broome in West Australia,' Maud told them. 'Across the Kimberley. It's fabulous country. You'd see thousands of rocks.'

'I'm sure we would, but we can't afford it,' Amy said, as Rachel looked bleak at all the rocks she'd miss. 'And my job starts the Monday after I reach Darwin.'

'But I'm not even sure Hugo can come now.' Maud was suddenly fretful. 'There's so much to do for the company. Now he's made the decision to take over…'

'He's doing that?' She shouldn't ask. She just sort of couldn't help herself.

'He is.' Maud sighed. 'He thinks he'll hate it, but it's the thought he hates. My James always said he'd be brilliant.' She cast a dubious glance at Amy. 'And he's started now, even though I'm sure he'd rather be here with y...with us.'

'We're coping beautifully without him,' Amy said, determinedly cheerful. 'It's been wonderful. Speaking of which...Rachel, would you like to sleep under the stars for our last night?'

'What, here?' Rachel looked at her as if she'd lost her mind.

'Grandma said it's magic,' Amy said. 'Sleeping outside in the desert.'

'Do you know how cold the desert gets at night?' Maud demanded, and Rachel shuddered.

'Chicken,' Amy said. 'Buster and I are game.'

'There are swags in the store,' Maud told her. 'But I'm not sure...'

'It'll be brilliant,' Amy said and thought: one more night to go, and if I go outside early enough it'll be one more night where I don't have to talk about—or think about—Hugo.

He'd been a bore. He'd hurt her. Hugo hadn't been at the company base for more than a couple of hours before he was seriously regretting what he'd done, and it was almost unbearable that Amy was at Natangarra while he was here.

But he'd made his decision, he told himself. He'd made two decisions. One, he needed to run this company. Two, he needed to do it alone. So get on with it.

At least the work pulled him in. By the end of the first day he found the adrenalin was running almost as high as it was in combat zones.

The company power brokers had flown in for the series of meetings happening while he was here. His grandfather had set these meetings up when he and Maud had booked the train journey, so Hugo was now here in his grandfather's place. But the suits, all affability on the outside, were far from pleased to see him.

There'd been conflict with his grandfather; he knew that. There'd been disagreements with a board who saw the company as pure profit-making, but the size of his grandfather's share-holdings meant he had the final say. That power was making the suits uneasy.

Their unease meant he needed to stop thinking of one slip of a girl and what she was doing without him.

Focus.

The company was negotiating a new mine, which

meant leasing more land. The suits were talking monetary compensation to the native landowners.

As he worked through the ramifications, the suits watched on the sidelines, gave him the figures he asked for and became more nervous.

Excellent.

On the second day he sat in the meeting with the tribal elders. For a while he stayed silent. He listened and he watched.

The elders were talking money with the suits, but their hearts weren't in it. They weren't objecting, though. The mines wouldn't harm their community. They were to be sited well away from settlements and the land would be restored when the company was done.

But these people didn't need more money, Hugo thought. He'd seen the figures.

In his head he reread one of his grandfather's last letters:

Thurstons is more than a company. The social conscience is what your grandmother and I have worked for. As majority shareholder, I can always influence direction. If you take over... That's what I dream of, Hugo. I know you don't want this life, but maybe this life wants you.

This life wants you...

Whether he wanted it or not, the decision had been made.

He was listening. He was thinking of Thurstons.

He was also thinking of Amy, of something Amy had said about her grandmother: *'She left as a kid, sent away to school and never got back...'*

So many of the native kids were caught between two cultures, he thought. So many of them left.

'Could we think outside the box?' he heard himself say, and the suits stared at him with disapproval. But Amy was suddenly there, front and centre. Amy's words.

Amy's people?

With Amy in his head, he wasn't about to be deflected by disapproval.

'I've been thinking maybe we have the opportunity to do something fantastic here,' he said, speaking to the elders and ignoring the stiffening of the suits. 'Your kids are currently using School of the Air, right? Which is great, but wouldn't a bricks and mortar school be better? But it'd need to be a school the kids would want to use. I'm thinking... What if we provide a school in payment for our lease of this further land? With the money we're talking, we could provide a swimming pool, gym, music facilities… We could bring in some great teachers, train them to help with what's important to you, make it wonderful.'

'That'd cost us a lot more than just a payout.' Thurstons' chief accountant sounded appalled, but the elders were suddenly far more interested.

'This is a long-term project,' Hugo said, thinking of the figures he'd worked on over the last twenty-four hours. 'But it's sustainable. From the company's point of view we'll have a community with skilled workers coming up. If our employees have kids in school, we'll have a more stable workforce. I can see long-term benefits all round.'

He could almost hear Maud and James behind him as he spoke—and Amy was there as well. The drift of outback kids to the city was inexorable. If he could slow it…

Amy would love this idea, he thought. He wanted to talk this through with her. She'd have suggestions. Maybe she could get involved.

Maybe…maybe…

The two days' absence was weakening his resolve. Was it weak to think he could take a risk? Ask her to take a risk?

She'd need the strength of Maud.

Back at Natangarra, he'd seen her beside Maud.

Maud was a big booming woman and Amy was petite and cute. He'd thought: no way.

But did strength come in size or in heart?

He thought of the women he'd worked beside in combat zones. Power wasn't necessarily proportionate to size.

She could throw a man. The memory still made him grin.

So maybe…

At the end of the day the elders left. They were deeply satisfied with what they'd achieved, and so was Hugo. The suits, not so much, but they'd accepted it.

They'd organised a corporate dinner. The plan was for the chopper to take him back to Natangarra the next morning—but he wanted to go home now.

Home to Amy. To ask her to take a risk?

He wasn't sure. To ask her to be so exposed… Was it fair?

He didn't know but, fair or not, he was going home to find out.

CHAPTER NINE

AT DUSK Amy carted her swag to the edge of the waterhole. Buster joined her for a while but, as the heat of the day faded and the cold of the desert night took over, he was torn. Outside and Amy, or inside with Rachel? As the temperature dropped, Rachel won.

'Wuss,' Amy called after him as he disappeared, but she didn't really mind. It was okay being alone. She snuggled into her swag and set herself to star watching.

She gazed up at the constellations her grandmother had taught her, and wondered how Bess could have born leaving here for the city. City stars were a faint shadow of these. This was awesome.

It was, however, cold. Her nose was icy.

No matter, she told herself. She'd promised herself she'd sleep under the stars and that was what she was doing.

A noise started, humming in from the south. A light…

A helicopter.

Hugo coming home? It had to be.

It had nothing to do with her, she told herself. The chopper landed on the paddock on the far side of the house to where she'd set her swag. A light went on in the house. The chopper took off again and disappeared into the night sky.

Hugo was home. So what?

She'd been trying to sleep. Now, however, she was wide awake.

Waiting?

For what? He didn't know she was here. It was midnight. He'd assume she'd be in the house, asleep.

She wriggled further down in the swag and told herself she was warm enough. She tried counting stars. She tried not to think about Hugo.

'Could you use a hot-water bottle?'

Her heart did a back-flip.

She hadn't heard him come. Maybe she'd even become airborne—she surely felt as if she'd landed with a thud.

'Do you…do you mind?'

'Do I mind what?' He was right beside her, squatting on his haunches, handing her a hot-water bottle. 'I thought you might need this. And more.' He had an armload of bedding. He draped it over the top of her swag without waiting for permission and then settled easily beside her, a man accustomed to settling in hard places.

'You weren't sleeping,' he said and it wasn't a question.

'No thanks to you,' she muttered. 'You scared me into the middle of next week.' It was a pretty efficient hot-water bottle, she thought. She was heating up really fast.

'It's a terrible spot for camping,' he said thoughtfully. 'In a hollow like this, anything could sneak up on you.'

'I'm not in Afghanistan.'

'No, you're not,' he said contentedly. 'Would you like a Tim Tam?'

He hauled open a packet of chocolate biscuits and handed one over. She was so disconcerted she took it without thinking.

Actually, disconcerted was a mild description for what she was feeling right now.

Hugo's hot-water bottle was delicious. She wriggled it down to her toes and felt the heat rise further.

She was holding a Tim Tam.

She ate it while she thought of what to say.

'How did you know I was out here?' she managed at last.

'Buster came out to greet me. He then raced out to the veranda, looked towards here and whined. Like he was torn. He obviously wasn't torn much, though, because he beetled straight back to Rachel's room. So I put my mighty powers of deduction to use and figured Rachel was in bed and you were here. Then I figured maybe I could do what Buster wouldn't do. I'd join you but I'd come prepared.'

'I…I quite like being by myself.' She swallowed her last mouthful of Tim Tam with an effort.

'But I find I don't,' he said gently. 'That's what this is about. I wanted you to be out here, so it was handy that you were in dire need.'

'I was not in dire need,' she said, trying to sound indignant, trying to ignore the first part of what he'd said. Surely it was a mistake. 'I…I was warm enough.'

'Liar. I've slept out here. I know how cold it gets.'

'I'm warm now,' she said, toasting her toes with

sensual pleasure, and then, because it was only polite, she ventured further. 'Did you have a good couple of days?'

'Excellent,' he told her. 'There's hot chocolate in this Thermos. You want some?'

'Is this a picnic?'

'Yes,' he said. 'Can I tell you what I've been doing?'

'Um…great,' she said because no other response seemed possible. She pushed herself up to sitting and draped one of the blankets Hugo had brought around her shoulders. Hugo poured chocolate.

They drank their hot chocolate and she felt… as if this night was taking her somewhere she'd never been before.

This man sitting beside her under a starlit sky.

She thought suddenly of her grandma, Bess, telling her about her love of the desert nights. Telling her of her love for her people.

Her people.

Bess would like Hugo, she thought, and then she thought: *what are you thinking?*

And then she decided it was too hard to think. She could just be. She could sit under the desert stars and let the night take her where it willed.

'I'd love you to tell me what you've been doing,' she said simply, and he did.

Many times Hugo had sat in the desert and watched the stars. Never with Amy.

If he had company he'd clam. He was known in the forces as a loner and he liked it that way.

He'd never felt the need to talk things through; could never see the point. But here, tonight, with Amy… Somehow talking to this woman seemed an extension of talking to himself.

Telling people your problems… He'd never understood it. It didn't make problems go away. Only tonight it sort of did. For two days he'd been thinking of Amy. He'd worked with her in his head. He'd made decisions and she'd been there in the process.

He wanted to talk to her now, of Thurston Holdings—*of his company*—how quickly it was feeling like that. He wanted to tell her of his meeting with the guys on the job, his awe at the organisation his grandfather had formed, his meeting with the tribal elders, his pride at what Thurstons could achieve. So yes, he'd wanted her to be awake when he got back.

She'd understand, he thought. She'd get what he was giving up; what he was moving into.

She'd made the same decision herself, only her future was more uncertain.

'That's great, Hugo,' she said when he'd talked himself out. 'I'm so glad it's working out for you.'

'I never wanted this,' he said simply. 'I ran from it. Now it's dragging me back and I'm thinking I can get real satisfaction from it.'

'And you'll do good things.'

'Part of it's from you,' he said simply. 'When we were sitting talking about the future of this place, suddenly…you were there. You and Rachel and your grandma. You helped.'

She stared at him in the moonlight, searching his face. 'Us…' she said at last.

'Your grandma belonged here,' he said softly. 'That's what I thought that maybe I could achieve. For the people who live here.' He hesitated. 'And even for myself. Maybe in her way, your grandma has helped me.'

There was a long and breathless silence. She didn't know where to take what he'd just said, he thought—and neither did he.

'So what will you do?' he asked finally into the

silence. 'Where do you belong, now that you've turned your back on the world you loved?'

'I'll teach.'

He frowned. 'Why? You could find another dance company. There are lots of companies out there without creeps like Ramón in them.'

She stilled. 'This…my future has nothing to do with Ramón.'

'Hasn't it?'

'I had to retire.'

'Hogwash,' he said crudely. 'I've watched you around Rachel. You wince and you move slowly, and you commiserate with Maud's aches and pains as if you have them as well. But you kept up with me at the Olgas. You rescued our joey—that leap left me stunned. You're no more arthritic than I am.'

'Hugo…'

'I've figured it,' he said. 'And I've done some research. You took time off when your sister first had the accident. Then you came back but in minor roles. I'm guessing Rachel needed you. But Ramón had been hurt, too, not much, but enough to stop him being leading man. Three months ago he blasted back and the arts media was full of him. I can only imagine how that felt—to dance behind him, to watch him when you know what he did to your sister… I read one interview when he even said the accident had been a good thing; it had forced him to concentrate on building his upper body strength. It had given him a break, he said, and he was glad it had happened. I can't imagine how that made you feel.'

She didn't respond. She gazed into the darkness. He could feel the tension in her, the anger.

And finally, finally, she said it like it was.

'I hated him,' she said simply. 'I went home every night to what he'd done to Rachel, and I wanted to make him suffer, too.' She shrugged. 'But that wouldn't help anyone. Rachel needed to get away. If I'd applied for another company… Rachel knows I was dancing for the best. She'd know why I was changing and she'd loathe it. And then these teaching jobs came up in Darwin: a great university role for Rachel and a position I thought I could be happy with. I knew Rachel wouldn't come alone. Her depression meant inertia and it was as much as I could do to make her apply. And she wouldn't let me come with her if she thought I was sacrificing my dancing because of it. I set it out as a new life for us both.'

'So you walked away entirely.'

'Ballet's not my life.'

'From what Maud says, it was.'

She shrugged. 'You can get satisfaction in different things. This teaching job sounds good.'

'But the waste...'

'Don't say it,' she said, and the anger was still there. 'It's my life, Hugo. I can belong...somewhere else.'

'And you'd make that sacrifice for Rachel?' Involuntarily he placed his arm round her shoulder and tugged her close. He half expected her to pull away. For a moment she stilled. She didn't speak for a long moment—and then she placed her hand over his. She leaned against him. The silence stretched out, and he knew something in her was letting go.

'You see the sacrifice because you're doing it, too,' she whispered. 'From desert isolation to the head of a financial empire... There are those who'd love it, but that's not you. But you do what you must because the alternative is too awful to think about. For now, though... We both need somehow to find a way to belong to where we land.'

More silence.

It wasn't an awkward silence, though. It was a silence that needed to happen, for them both to figure the next step.

If there was a next step.

'You must be cold,' she said at last, and he thought about that, thought about the implications.

'I'm tough.' But he didn't feel tough.

'Tough but cold?'

'I'll go back to the house when I'm cold.'

'This swag's pretty big. You could...share.'

There was another stillness then, but it was a different stillness. The parameters were changing.

She was still leaning against him. The link suddenly seemed stronger. Stronger and more urgent.

'I'm just offering,' she said simply into the silence. 'I know we can't have anything long term, but we're mature adults. Maybe for tonight...'

'For tonight?'

'For tonight, you've brought me blankets and heat and Tim Tams,' she said simply. 'Those things are wonderful—but I want more.'

'Amy...'

'But you know there's something else we need.'

She sounded unsure then, as if suddenly doubting her own temerity. 'I...I don't carry them,' she said. 'I know I should but, believe it or not, I...I didn't see this coming.'

He didn't say anything. He couldn't. She'd taken his breath away. What he wanted too much...she was simply offering.

'I don't usually make this sort of suggestion,' she whispered. 'In truth, I never have. Maybe it's crazy, maybe it's immoral, maybe it's both. But there's something about this night. There's something about you. Hugo, I'm not asking more of you than you want to give, but for now...if you happen to be a man who comes prepared...' She took a deep breath. 'Hugo, for now, for this night, I belong here. And I want you.'

And what was a man to say to that?

I don't usually...

He knew truth when he heard it. This was as out of character for Amy as it was for him.

I didn't see this coming.

This need. This magnetic force. This coming together of two halves of a whole.

Maybe he had seen it coming. Maybe this night had been in his head for two days.

He'd brought condoms.

I don't usually... she'd said.

There was nothing usual about this night.

She'd tugged away, out of his hold, so she could read his face. She was meeting his gaze in the starlight, directly, honestly, her gaze telling him she wanted him as a woman wanted a man, with a need as ancient as time itself.

He met her gaze and his heart twisted. A night under the stars. A woman as lovely as Amy. An offer he couldn't believe she'd made.

But maybe the offer had been inevitable. No matter which one of them had brought it up, that was how it felt. Inevitable and right.

I belong here.

He slipped his fingers into her tousled curls. He drew her tenderly towards him and he kissed her.

This was a gift with a value beyond measure.

He held her in his arms and his world shifted.

He let himself fall in love.

Dawn crept over the horizon with a stealth and beauty that took her breath away.

She was lying spooned against Hugo's body. She was warm, sated and happy—as warm, sated and happy as a woman could be.

The cat with the cream. That was how she felt.

She could see Uluru in the distance, a great gilded glow, shimmering in dawn-tinged light. The desert between here and the horizon was vast and breathtaking.

This was her grandmother's country. It was her country. She belonged here.

She belonged in this man's arms.

She'd never felt as whole as she'd felt last night. Making love with Hugo felt as if two halves of a whole had finally found their rightful place.

He'd joined with her and her head had felt as if it must surely explode. She'd never known such joy. But now, afterwards, in the rising dawn, the peace she knew was profound and wonderful.

She was home, in the arms of the man she loved. Loved?

She'd known him for less than a week.

But she did know him, she thought, as she felt him stir and his arms tightened around her. Skin to skin…nothing could feel this wonderful. If this was all there was, she thought, if he walked away from this moment, she could never regret this night. She'd walked into this with her eyes wide open.

He was her outback warrior and she gloried in

it. She gloried in him. He was about to be thrust into a life he loathed, but he'd enter that life with strength and with honour.

And somehow… Somehow he'd fed her strength. She had a new life, too, that she was about to step into. It terrified her—life without her dancing—but if this man could do what he must alone, then so could she.

She'd taken strength from him, she thought, and she smiled.

'What's funny?' He was cradling her, holding her with such tenderness… He'd heard her smile?

'I was just hoping I'm not Delilah,' she whispered into the dawn. 'Taking your strength for my own.'

'You haven't,' he murmured in mock horror. He raked his hair, flinching with pretend horror. 'My ponytail…woman, where is it?'

'Eat Tim Tams,' she said equably. 'Food to make it grow back. It's the only thing to do.'

'No,' he murmured, nuzzling her ear. 'It's not the only thing to do. If I can just gather my failing strength…'

'Try,' she said, and he did.

With joy.

* * *

You'd think, Hugo decided wryly, that at six o'clock in the morning a man could have a bit of privacy in his own house. Instead, as he and Amy slipped in the back entrance, hoping to make it to their respective bedrooms unnoticed, they found the entire household assembled in the kitchen. Maudie, Rachel, Wendy, Scott, Scott's two kelpies and Buster.

That made seven sets of eyes. Hugo ushered Amy in from the back porch and every set was on them.

'About time,' Maud said. 'I was about to send Wendy down with pancakes.'

Pancakes. He checked the kitchen table and saw a mound that'd do a battalion credit.

'We thought you might be hungry,' Maud said. 'We all are.'

Wendy and Scott were dressed. Rachel and Maud were in dressing gowns.

They were all—including the dogs—looking pleased with themselves.

Wendy was pouring coffee, as if finally they'd arrived for a scheduled breakfast.

They were expected to calmly sit down at the breakfast table and drink coffee?

What else to do?

Amy grinned and sat. She'd worn her custom-ary leggings and baggy sweater out to the water-hole and she was wearing them again now. She looked, though…well, rumpled wouldn't begin to describe it.

She looked loved, Hugo thought, watching the faint colour tinge her cheeks as she concentrated fiercely on spooning sugar into her mug.

He didn't remember her having sugar.

'The stars were great,' she said, sounding a bit breathless. 'It was an awesome night.'

'I'm glad my grandson was able to share it with you,' Maud said, and her satisfaction was unmis-takable and profound.

Uh oh. Maudie in full cry. He might just as well have produced a diamond.

He glanced at Amy and caught her glancing back at him. She looked away fast and started stir-ring her coffee. She was starting to lose her glow.

Woman caught after a one-night stand?

'It was an awesome night,' he repeated, sol-idly and surely. He sat and loaded a plate with pancakes, then looked across at Amy and kept on looking until finally she looked up and met his gaze. 'It was pretty much the most wonderful night of my life,' he said. 'I never knew star-gazing could be so amazing.'

She blushed—but he saw the beginnings of a smile. She wasn't being treated as a one-night stand. What had happened between them had been momentous and he was acknowledging it.

'Scott offered to take Rachel bird-watching at dawn,' Maud said to the room in general. 'But they decided it was too cold.'

And the birds would be around the waterhole, Hugo thought. Good one, Scott.

Scott was grinning. He was a weather-beaten, taciturn farm manager. Hugo had never seen him grin in his life.

'It wasn't a good morning for disturbing the wildlife,' he said. 'Rachel decided to sort a few rocks instead.'

And Rachel smiled at Amy, took pity on her and launched into her best professorial tone. Yes, she'd been sorting rocks. They were amazing samples. Did they know Uluru and Kata Tjuta were built from sandstone, deposited when Australia was an inland sea, but some seismic event had tipped and changed their structure? She was trying to work out if it was the one event or many. There was controversy. Did they know Professor Ernest Mathison of the University of…

She kept going happily, trying not to grin.

Amy's colour finally subsided. She drank her coffee—though Hugo saw her wince as she realised how much sugar was in it.

She glanced up and he grinned at her and winked, and she blushed all over again.

'Tell me about Professor Mathison,' Hugo said encouragingly to Rachel. 'Is he a rival?'

Rachel glanced again at Amy and her smile widened. *Was this the depressed Rachel of only days ago?*

'Yes, he is,' she said. 'Do you want to hear the stupidity of his thesis?'

'Yes,' Hugo said. 'I believe we do.'

'Of course you do,' Maud said. 'And then you can tell us all about what happens at an outback waterhole at dawn.'

'In your dreams,' Hugo said and everyone laughed.

Even Amy.

Too soon, it was time to leave, time to drive back to Alice Springs and catch the *Ghan* again.

Amy sat in the back of the car with Rachel and Buster and let the others do the talking.

Maud and Rachel were chattering like new best friends. Hugo was responding every now and then, his lovely deep voice making her toes curl.

Amy was trying to figure how to get on with her life.

She had to get her toes uncurled. No matter that Hugo had loved her as much as she'd loved him, no matter that he'd treated her with respect, this had to stop. They were poles apart.

They had twenty-four more hours on the train and then it was over.

Hugo and Maud had tickets on a cruise boat travelling from Darwin to Broome. She and Rachel had an apartment booked in Darwin. She'd start her new job. Life would resume a new normal.

But…but…

She felt loved.

Every time Hugo spoke she felt loved. Even when he was talking rocks to Rachel… Even when he was talking business with Maud…

He feels like mine, she thought, and for a little, for just a little, she hugged Buster and she let herself dream. She let herself believe that this was a fairy tale where a wand could be waved and somehow a billionaire warrior could want an out-of-date ballet dancer and there'd be a happy ever after.

In her dreams.

Right, she thought, but the drive was long and she was weary and there was nothing wrong with curling up in the back of the gorgeous car and letting her dreams take her where they willed.

She'd wake up soon enough.

She did.

CHAPTER TEN

WAKING from dreams was never easy. Waking was not, however, usually so hard.

They arrived at Alice Springs Railway Station. An official from Hugo's company was there to collect the car. He smiled a formal greeting to Maud and to Rachel, but when he saw Amy he grinned.

'I'm very pleased to meet you,' he said, and it was as if he knew all about her and had been hoping to meet her for some time.

His greeting made her uneasy.

The station was busy. The *Ghan* had arrived earlier in the day. Passengers going all the way through to Darwin had left the train and spent a few hours exploring Alice Springs. Others, like them, were rejoining the train after a break. There were people everywhere.

Most of them were glancing, covertly or not so covertly, at Amy.

Why?

Had Buster stuck his head out?

No.

The little dog was safely back in her purse, and he shouldn't be a problem this time. She and Rachel would be in one of the sumptuous Platinum carriages. And as well as that... 'If we need to grease palms we'll grease them,' Hugo had said. 'No more midnight dashes in your pyjamas.'

She'd arrived at the station thinking this was going to be easy. Now, though...

Why was everyone looking at her?

People were also looking at Hugo, but she could understand that. As one of Australia's mega-rich, he'd command attention even if he wasn't drop-dead gorgeous, and his picture had been in the tabloids recently as speculation grew about Thurstons.

People were looking at Maud, too. Maud was known and respected throughout the country.

But Amy...

'Have I got a hole in my tights?' she muttered to Rachel and Rachel shook her head, clearly as puzzled as she was.

Hugo's associate—Raymond—was helping them

with the suitcases. Their little group was the centre of interest for the entire precinct.

And then all was explained. Inside the station doors was a news-stand, and in front were billboards. Big billboards. Three billboards for three different publications.

The same photograph on each.

Five nights ago. Amy and Hugo, on the train.

Hugo was holding her shoulders. Her face was tilted to his, he was looking at her, and the way he was looking at her… A kiss was inevitable. His look was a kiss in itself.

At least Hugo was dressed, Amy thought, feeling appalled. She was wearing her pink pyjamas. Her hair was tousled. She looked as if she'd just stepped out of the bathroom—into the arms of her lover?

'*Mystery Pyjama Girl,*' the caption blazed. '*Capturing the Thurston Billions?*'

She felt sick.

Hugo's arm came round her, moving his body between her and the crowd. 'Get back.'

But it was too late. 'You're the pyjama girl,' someone yelled at her, and cameras appeared from everywhere. The press had obviously been waiting. Every passenger seemed to have their cell-phone camera.

Hugo had no hope of hiding her.

She felt every vestige of colour drain from her body. She pushed back from Hugo, thinking no, she wanted no part of this.

But then…

Then it wasn't up to her. He let her go, no, more than that, he was putting her away, propelling her towards Rachel.

'Shield your sister and move away from us,' he told Rachel in a voice she didn't recognise. It was a commander voice, clipped and harsh. 'Hide your faces. If we stay together it'll get worse. Move your hands back and forth so photos will blur. Raymond, look after them. Maud, come with me. Get on the train, fast.'

And he was gone, striding roughly through the crowd, propelling Maud in front of him.

With Hugo gone, the photographers weren't sure what to do, but they kept on clicking as the reporters moved in.

'Can you tell us your name? Are you and Major Thurston an item? How long have you been seeing him? Is he taking over Thurston Holdings?

He's booked from Darwin on a cruise with his grandmother. Are you going, too?'

'We haven't seen you in society circles,' someone else yelled. 'Are you Australian?'

She couldn't answer. This was worse than appalling, she thought as Rachel shielded her as best she could and Raymond steered them towards the train. This was a vortex, about to suck her in.

Hugo hated publicity. She'd landed him in it. But then, she thought, she'd landed herself in it. Compared to her, in the photo Hugo looked almost respectable. *And he'd walked away?*

She was the one who'd been caught in the train corridor in pink pyjamas.

She couldn't be angry. Hugo had been helping save her dog, she told herself. But still…it hurt, that he was striding away, leaving her to face this alone.

And Rachel was wilting.

They needed to get on the train.

'Run for it,' Raymond said grimly.

They ran.

He felt cold and sick and tired. Hugo ushered Maud onto the train and he thought: that's that. Over.

'Why did you leave them?' Maud had found herself propelled onto the train, into their cabin, almost before she knew what had happened and she sounded stunned.

'I don't want photographs of me with Amy. It'll feed the frenzy.'

'It will,' Maud agreed, but she was already eyeing her grandson with disapproval. 'But you need to face them some time.'

'Why?'

'Because you and Amy…'

'There is no *me and Amy*,' Hugo snapped and his grandmother stilled.

'So last night…you made love to her and now you're walking away?'

She'd guessed, Hugo thought bleakly. Of course she'd guessed.

'Last night was a mistake.'

What had he been thinking? He'd seen Amy's face as she saw the billboards. For all her bravado about the way he should face the press, when it came to reality she'd come close to collapse. How had he ever thought he could do that to her? 'I was looking for something I can't have,' he said.

'So have you told Amy last night was a mistake?'

'This is my…'

'Don't you dare say this is not my business,' she snapped. 'Amy's lovely. I won't have you treating her like a tramp.'

'She is lovely,' Hugo agreed. 'That's why last night happened but it shouldn't have. That's why I need to walk away.'

'So you'll write her a polite note?' She was practically seething.

'I'll talk to her, but not on this train.'

'So how do you think she's feeling now?'

'Exposed,' he snapped. 'She's been photographed in her pyjamas, and that photograph will be spread all over Australia. You know what that sort of publicity causes.'

'No,' Maud said carefully. 'Tell me.'

He gritted his teeth, wanting to shut up, wanting to retreat. Maud was probably the only person in the world who'd make him answer.

'You've watched my father's women,' he said. 'You saw what happened. My mother… All the rest… So many.'

'Your father was a fool,' Maud snapped. 'And his women… They didn't handle the media spotlight well.'

'Well? Are you kidding? It destroyed them.'

'It didn't destroy me.'

'You were introduced to it gradually and you're different. You have strength.'

'You're saying,' Maud said cautiously, 'that because I'm six feet tall and toughened by years of exposure, I can handle the media, and because Amy's five feet four and cute and blonde, she can't.'

'Yes!' He groaned. 'You saw her face when she saw the billboards. She loathed it.'

'So she needs to find a respectable wrap when she wears pyjamas on trains. You're being insulting.'

'I'm being realistic.'

'You're shooting yourself in the foot,' Maud said darkly. 'Not giving her a chance.'

'Grandma, I've told you I'm quitting the army,' Hugo said wearily. 'I've told you I'll take on this lifestyle, but I don't have to drag anyone else into it.'

'Maybe she wouldn't have to be dragged. Amy's special. You know she is.'

'Maybe she is,' Hugo said. 'And maybe that's why I won't destroy her.'

* * *

Their cabin was Platinum Class, as promised, and it was almost as sumptuous as the one Maud and Hugo had used on the Adelaide-Alice Springs run.

They had vast picture windows to watch the desert. They had room service. They could batten down and stay put. Which was just as well, Amy thought. She'd heard the talk as the Platinum butler showed them to their cabin. Everyone who saw them was asking the same.

'That's Thurston's pyjama girl. Who is she?'

A newspaper was provided in their cabin and she read the article with disbelief.

The caption read: *'Who's PJ?'*

Major Hugo Thurston, heir to the Thurston empire, is currently travelling north on the Ghan. *He was photographed five nights ago in a midnight assignation with an unknown pyjama girl. Who is this woman who's attracted the attention of Australia's most eligible bachelor?*

Luckily the photo wasn't great. Hugo was in focus but Amy wasn't. Her curls hadn't been combed after washing and they were drifting over her face. When she was dancing she wore her hair groomed tightly back. From this picture, she doubted anyone in her dancing world would recognise her.

Back at the station… She and Rachel had covered their faces as soon as they'd realised cameras were pointing at them. Raymond had shielded them. Maybe the anonymous pyjama girl could stay anonymous.

Maybe her pyjamas wouldn't have consequences.

They already had had consequences.

She looked at the picture again and winced. *Woman who's attracted the attention of Australia's most eligible bachelor…* Maybe Hugo was right to stride away the moment the press appeared.

Maybe he was but it didn't make her feel good.

'I wonder where they are,' Rachel said, and Amy sighed. *They.* The two new people in Rachel's life. Maud and Hugo had made Rachel happy. She should be grateful, but right now she was thinking of Hugo as he strode away and she wasn't feeling grateful at all.

'I suspect he saw this picture and decided the peasants are revolting,' she ventured.

Rachel smiled. 'Hugo's not like that. You know

he's not. He's treated us as equals from the start. He's gorgeous, Ames.'

'And you of all people know where gorgeous gets you,' Amy said shortly. 'Didn't we make a vow about falling...'

'We made a vow not to be stupid,' Rachel retorted. 'Falling for Hugo's not stupid.'

'It is if he doesn't want me.' There, it was said, loud and clear. The words hung between them as the full import of what she'd admitted sank in.

At their feet, Buster was examining his new quarters with enthusiasm. He was obviously a dog who approved of luxury.

Not Amy.

'This is Hugo's world,' Amy whispered. 'It's not my world. I'm the unknown pyjama girl on the front of the newspaper.'

'You're better than that,' Rachel said and hugged her. 'Hugo knows you're special.'

'He feels exposed,' she said. 'I know he does. And to have someone with him...someone like the pyjama girl...that'll make him even more exposed.'

'But if he loves you...'

'No,' she said, hauling herself together, trying to think logically. Last night Hugo had fed her strength and she'd done the same for him, but there'd been no commitment. There wasn't a need for commitment. They were moving in separate directions. She hadn't expected the separation to happen quite so soon, but it did have to happen. So why not now?

'We had a great time,' she said, picking Buster up and hugging him. 'It was an awesome adventure, but Hugo Thurston's pyjama girl is not who I am. I'm Amy Cotton, sister to Rachel, half mum to Buster, and we're on the *Ghan* and we're heading for the next amazing part of our lives.'

'Without Maud?' Rachel said in a small voice. 'And without Hugo?'

'Without the Thurstons,' Amy said. 'Exactly.'

Maud bullied Hugo back to the dining car for meals but Rachel and Amy didn't show.

It was just as well, Hugo thought grimly. The eyes of half the people on this train were watching. If Amy appeared…even if she sat at the other end of the dining car to him…there'd be photographs taken.

Of his pyjama girl.

Who was she? The tabloids were demanding an answer. Thankfully, the *Ghan* had strict policies about releasing passenger details. If she kept to herself for the rest of the trip, if she and Rachel got a cab away from the station when they reached Darwin and went in the opposite direction to him, this whole media fuss would die down.

'Ask them to join us in our cabin,' Maud demanded after dinner and he shook his head.

'Maud, you of all people know what the media is like. They'll be paying people to watch.'

'Then it serves you right for being so interesting,' Maud snapped. 'You should have married a mousey girl with dubious clothes sense fifteen years ago. Instead of which, you disappear, you turn into a commando, you come home as a billionaire and unattached... Of course the media's interested. Just be boring.'

'I am being boring. I'll play Scrabble with you and go to bed.'

'Don't be a fool.'

'It's not foolish to figure I'm not dragging anyone else into this life.'

'It didn't kill me. Or James.' Maud allowed herself a wintry smile. 'Sometimes we even enjoyed it.'

'You were born strong and you grew stronger.'

'You won't give Amy the benefit of the doubt and assume she can be just as strong?'

'You saw her cringe when she saw the posters.'

'I'd cringe, too, if I faced photographers in my pyjamas. You'll get better at avoiding that nonsense. Hire the girl a hairdresser. Spend some serious money on clothes.'

'Turn her into one of my father's bimbos?'

'Are you saying,' Maud said carefully, 'that you're equating hairdressers and clothes with your father's women? I've spent serious money on clothes and hairdressers, I've enjoyed every minute of it and I don't believe for one moment that I'm a bimbo. And to equate Amy…that's almost as insulting. She has strength. She'll learn how to cope with the media, as will you.'

'I need to. She doesn't.'

'She does if she wants to share your life.'

'I won't ask it of her.'

'And she gets no say?'

'Dammit, Grandma, I haven't even figured how I'm going to cope with this life myself yet,' he exploded. 'It's far too soon to be dragging a woman into it as well.'

'If you're thinking of dragging Amy anywhere…'

'No,' he said and raked his hair. His hair was getting pretty severely raked right now. 'I'm not.'

'She won't be dragged. She's one amazing woman.'

'She is, but I don't need a woman.'

'Liar,' Maud said and gave him a really disgusted look and went to bed.

Playing Scrabble by yourself was pretty much impossible.

He cheated. He reported himself to himself, disqualified himself and tried to read. His crime thriller hadn't grown any more thrilling since the last time he'd tried.

He did some desultory work on his laptop. It grew more and more desultory.

Somewhere in this carriage was Amy. It wouldn't be so hard to find her.

The butler would probably have a cellphone camera and there'd be more problems.

Yeah, but… But…

He sat and stared at the Scrabble board—and saw Amy.

A knock. Amy? He was on his feet by the second rap, only to hear a man's voice. 'Major Thurston?'

He shoved back a slump of disappointment and opened the door to the Platinum butler.

'I have a message,' the man said, trying to sound bland and official. 'From Miss Cotton. She says…' He hesitated, as if he wasn't sure he had the message right. As if he couldn't believe the message. 'She says you have her steak sandwich. I've offered her another from cabin service but she seems to think the…the sandwich you have is preferable. Would you like me to take it to her, sir?'

Despite his attempt to sound official, the man looked astounded, even disdainful, and Hugo came close to grinning as he realised what Amy wanted.

He'd packed Buster's dog food into his kitbag when they'd left Uluru. He'd forgotten about it. Buster would be hungry.

Some things couldn't be tolerated. Buster. Hunger. Before he could think of sense and prudence, he heard himself offer, 'I'll take it to her.'

Hang on a minute. Wasn't that what he'd vowed not to do?

Whatever. A man had to do what a man had to do. Buster without food was an emergency.

'We have sandwiches on board,' the man said stiffly.

'But our cook back at Uluru makes gourmet sandwiches,' Hugo told him. 'You can't compete. Tell me what cabin she's in.'

This made sense, he told himself. It was late. Almost everyone was in their cabins with the door shut. He could give the dog food to her and leave.

He thought of her face back at Alice Springs as she'd seen the billboards. He needed to apologise.

Tomorrow the journey would be over and she'd be gone. The thought of seeing her one last time was irresistible.

Amy opened the door with caution, expecting the po-faced butler and a parcel of dog food—but it was Hugo. He was right in the doorway, big and weathered and…Hugo.

She took an involuntary step back.

He didn't follow her in. He simply stood in the doorway and waited for her to collect herself.

At least she wasn't in pyjamas this time, she thought wildly. She had more sense.

She shouldn't even have contacted him. She'd fed Buster a little of their dinner but Buster was a creature of habit. Titbits were titbits and dinner was dinner, and he wouldn't sleep without a proper meal. And they'd need the dog food tomorrow. 'Go get it,' Rachel had said, but Amy had more sense than that. She'd sent the butler.

And got Hugo instead.

'Dinner, m'lady?' Hugo said, smiling that gorgeous sardonic smile that had her heart doing back-flips.

'Thank you,' she said, feeling panicked. She grabbed the parcel and tried to shut the door.

He moved in, just a little, just enough to make it impossible to close him out.

'I'm sorry,' he said.

'For hanging onto Buster's food?' she managed. 'So you should be.'

'For the media hype. For the pyjamas.'

'It wasn't your fault. I'm the one who wore pink satin.'

'They wouldn't have taken the picture if you hadn't been with me.'

'No,' she said. 'They wouldn't.'

'That's why I left you on the platform,' he said. 'We don't want to give them any more fodder.'

'Don't *we*?'

He paused. 'Maybe *we* do,' he said at last, in a voice she didn't recognise. 'Maybe you'd like publicity.'

She froze. 'You think I like being photographed in pyjamas?'

He thought back to all the women his father had dated. He thought for just a moment too long.

'You do,' she muttered and tried again to haul the door closed.

'Amy, I'm sorry.'

'I'm sorry, too. Let me close the door.'

'Let me come in.'

'No way. Someone might see. There'll be a picture of a closed door in tomorrow's papers.'

'You're right. There would be.'

'So what?' It was almost a yell, and he did step back. She hauled at the door, but he shoved his foot in before she succeeded.

'Amy, you don't want this life.'

What was he talking about? 'Platinum?' she demanded, glancing behind her at the plush furnishings. 'Of course I don't. What can I have been thinking? Cattle class is for the likes of me.'

'That's not what I meant.'

'What did you mean?'

'If you and I took things further...'

'That's weird.' Anger was coming to her aid now, fury plain and simple. 'I thought we already did take it further. How much further can I go than sleeping with you?'

All the doors in the corridor were closed. Maybe no one could hear, but if they could, maybe she didn't care. The moment at the station where he'd seen the image on the billboards and walked away fast… It hurt. It hurt still.

She didn't expect anything of this man, she told herself. She'd asked for no long-term commitment, but having him turn his back on her and walk away had made her feel desolate.

Because she had expected something of him. That was the problem, she thought. Their intimacy last night had led her down a whole different path. She'd allowed herself to dream.

'If we married…' he said and there was that path rising up in front of her, or maybe it wasn't a path but more of a gaping hole. The way he said it…

'You think that's what I want?' she breathed. 'You think I'm trying to trap you into *marriage*?'

'Of course I don't. Amy…'

'Let me close the door,' she said icily. 'Thank you for bringing Buster's food. Thank you for your hospitality at Uluru. Now leave.'

'If we take it further it'll destroy you,' he said

flatly, and she looked into his face and saw a tension that was almost unbearable.

He believed it, she thought. He looked…torn.

'You'd destroy me?' she asked at last. 'You, personally?'

'The media. The lifestyle.'

'Champagne and caviar.' She was having trouble understanding. She was having trouble breathing. 'I can see that it might.'

'Amy…'

Anger was still helping her, and suddenly something else. Her background. Her grandma. The things that made her what she was.

'My grandma was a Koori who lived out here on the land,' she said, softer now, anger and confusion fading to a bleak desolation. And betrayal? 'That's about as far from your world as it's possible to be. The rest of me comes from farming stock. Pig farmers, if you must know. None of this landed gentry for yours truly. So if you want a woman…yes, it'd be better to choose someone with blue blood heritage, but as for destroying…'

'This has nothing to do with your heritage,' he snapped.

'Then what?'

'You have no idea of the life. You know the corporation I'll be leading. You know the money I control. Being my wife…'

'See, that's what I don't get,' she managed. 'The wife thing. When did that happen? I thought we were one time lovers?'

'We are.'

'So who's talking about wives?'

'If I was free,' he said, and it was as if the words were torn from him, 'I'd marry you in a heart-beat.'

Whoa.

She took a deep breath. Tried desperately to re-group. Tried to meet him on his terms. 'Why?' she said at last and her words sounded strangled even to her.

'Because you're like no woman I've ever met,' he said simply. 'You're brave and loyal and feisty. You've given up what you love most in the world to help your sister. You're devoted to a dog even his mother would have trouble loving. You make Maud laugh and you make me laugh. You're more beautiful than any woman I've ever met—and when I touch you I burn.'

Breathless didn't begin to describe how she was feeling right now. Her breath had been vacuumed right out of her. 'Is that right?' she whispered.

'You…you think you want to marry me—yet you walk away?'

'I will not bring another woman into this life.'

It was said with such anger and such conviction that she knew it for truth. His bleakness frightened her.

I will not bring another woman into this life…

She thought of the stories she'd heard of his father's womanising. Of the streams of disasters. Of the childhood this man must have endured.

Hugo was who he was for a reason, she thought bleakly. He was a loner. He wouldn't risk—and she couldn't ask him to risk.

What was more, she wasn't sure she wanted to.

Last night had been crazy. She'd thrown herself at him and it all seemed a dream. And now? Maybe he was right. If she stepped forward and clung, within months she might be deeply regretting it.

'You're right, of course,' she managed. 'I don't know your world, so I wouldn't know. That cringing thing back at the station—that was sadly out of character. I bet if I had the slightest chance, I'd step into the spotlight and like it. I'd wear stilettos and sequins and buy myself a cleavage. I'd drink

Martinis for breakfast and have my own personal masseur. I'd…'

'I know you wouldn't,' he said steadily. 'But some of the women my father introduced to his lifestyle did go down that path, and for them…'

She knew the gossip. In ballet circles, everything to do with the Thurstons was legitimate fodder and his father's death had dragged it all out again.

'They talked of your father's women in ballet circles,' she said. 'I heard one suicided. One even retreated to a nunnery. So that's your problem? You like me but you don't want me to face the choice between cocaine or the cloisters. Hmm. I expect I should be grateful for your concern.' She took a deep breath. Steadied. 'Well…I guess that's that. Thank you, Hugo, and thank you also for the dog food. Now, can you take your foot out of my door and let me go to bed?'

'Amy…'

'Hugo,' she said flatly, angrily. 'Let's stop this right now. I'm not deciding between suicide or the cloisters. Neither am I deciding about you. We had a great time last night. The sex was awesome. I'll remember it for ever but that's all it was. One night. Great sex. And now, I'm not risking a nunnery and you're not asking me to. Goodnight, Hugo.'

And before he guessed what she intended, she flicked her foot at his, hard. Her shoe caught his shin, just above his ankle. He jerked back and the door was shut in his face.

Martial arts…

Never fall for a woman who could fight back.

Never fall for a woman.

He stared at the closed door. Any minute now, another of these doors could open. He'd be seen, photographed looking like an idiot.

An idiot for Amy?

A commando who'd just been given his marching orders.

It was he who'd made the decision, he thought. He'd seen her face when he'd mentioned marriage. He'd seen the flare of shock, but he'd also seen something else. Something that might almost be longing?

He must have imagined it, but even if he hadn't…

She couldn't want his world. He didn't even know it himself. He had no right to drag her into it with him.

But then… Amy Cotton wasn't a woman to be

dragged anywhere, he thought, wincing at the pain in his ankle. If he just asked…

No.

Alone, he could control things, he thought. He could refuse to let the media get to him. He could retreat into isolation when things got tough.

With Amy, he'd be exposed from every side.

Last night had been a gigantic mistake. Falling for Amy had been a gigantic mistake.

He couldn't make it up to her. All he could do for her now was walk away.

Move on.

What next?

The *Ghan* was due to reach Darwin the next day, but the holiday he'd agreed to take Maud on didn't stop there. They were due to board a cruise boat, exploring the vast North Australian coastline.

They had ten days in Darwin first, and Amy was staying in Darwin.

Darwin was a small city and, the way Hugo was feeling, New York would be too small.

But…he'd received a message just before he'd left Uluru. The company was facing a crisis with an environmental spill down south. Left to their own devices, he suspected the managers would hush it up, go into damage control.

Hushed up, the environmental damage could be enormous.

Maud had friends in Darwin. He could leave her with them and spend the week coping with the spill. It'd be hands-on experience.

The Barstock mine was in rough country. The living would be hard.

Excellent. He could live rough for a while. He could get his head back into working order.

Soft beds... Platinum service... After twenty years in the army, they were doing his head in.

Amy was doing his head in.

'Amy?'

Amy leaned against the door and breathed deeply. Rachel was watching her from her bed. She was hugging Buster and they were both looking deeply worried.

'A compartment in a train's too small for personal stuff,' Rachel said softly. 'I'm sorry, but there's no way we could avoid hearing. Buster's shocked to the socks.'

Buster did look shocked. She fed him his dinner and he stopped looking shocked, but Rachel still did.

'You guys were talking of marriage?'

'Not me,' she said, trying to sound flippant. 'And he only said he'd like to marry me if the world changed. That's hardly a proposal.'

'He loves you, Ames.'

'He doesn't know what he loves. He's a loner. I shouldn't have got involved.'

'But you're in love with him,' Rachel said on a note of discovery. 'Oh, Ames…'

'If I am, then I'm stupid,' she said. 'Stupid, stupid, stupid. Like you and Ramón. We're two of a kind.'

'Kind isn't a word that could ever describe Ramón,' Rachel said stoutly. 'Hugo's nothing like him.'

'No. Ramón's a media whore. Compared to him, Hugo's a hermit. A hermit who doesn't want any pink satin pyjama girl on his arm.'

'You could…I don't know…wear black? Black's classy.'

'Black PJs?'

'You're classy whatever you wear,' Rachel said stoutly, and proceeded to hug her. 'Oh, Ames, what will you do?'

'What you're doing, I guess,' Amy said. 'Settle down in Darwin. Get on with my life.'

'And if the media discovers you're PJ?'

'I'll be a one day wonder.'

'While Hugo moves on to his next woman?'

'Or no woman at all,' Amy said and sat on the bed and felt ill. Not ill for her. Ill for Hugo. He had everything, she thought, and he had nothing.

CHAPTER ELEVEN

HUGO spent a week in the desert. He learned about spillage and environmental containment. To the astonishment of the management, he threw himself into hard physical work alongside the men. His men. His company.

He tried to get his head back together.

At the end of the week he had the situation in hand, he had the men's respect—but Amy was still in his head, front and centre.

It couldn't matter. He flew back to Darwin thinking she'd be settled somewhere and he didn't need to know where. He must move on.

He landed at Darwin Airport, he strolled through the terminal—and he stopped dead.

Another billboard. Another headline.

'Thurston's Pyjama Girl, Dancing Tonight. Introducing PJ!'

Maud had been staying with her friends, and that was where he headed. Harold and Margaret lived on the headland overlooking Darwin harbour, in one of the most expensive pieces of real estate in town. He spent the whole cab ride there seething.

But his grandmother was bubbling with so much excitement she didn't notice his mood. She greeted him with an exuberance he hadn't seen since James had died.

'We're having an early dinner,' she told him, practically bouncing as she dragged him indoors. 'I'm so pleased your plane wasn't late. We have tickets.'

'Where are you going?' This was his bereaved grandmother? She looked a different woman.

'To Amy's concert, of course. The theatre's on the other side of the city, so we need to leave soon. It was supposed to be in the school hall but they've had to shift it. Even now I gather it's standing room only. Harold had to use his position with the bank to get us tickets. I don't usually approve of pulling strings—*but this is Amy.*'

'You're going to see Amy?'

'We all are,' she told him, seemingly bemused at his obvious confusion. She led him into the sitting room to where his hosts were waiting, but he scarcely noticed.

Maybe Amy had been in the papers every day since he'd left, he thought, stunned. There hadn't been a lot of newspapers where he'd been.

What was going on?

'Dinner's in ten minutes,' Maud was saying. 'And then...'

'I'm not going to see Amy Cotton make money out of tabloid gossip!' It was an explosion, and Harold and Margaret and Maud all took a step back.

Harold headed one of Australia's largest banks. Margaret was head of a huge arts foundation. They were powerful people and they'd been Maud's friends for a long time. They looked at Maud in concern. They looked at Hugo and they stepped forward again, as if they were about to protect her from her grandson.

It needed only this. As if he'd do violence to Maud.

'I have no idea why you're going,' he said through gritted teeth, 'but count me out.'

'Hugo, you will support Amy.'

Very few people heard Maud's voice as it sounded now but, once heard, respect was gained for life. It sounded like blasted cannonballs, each word a force exploding into the universe to change things.

Why? Hugo stared at her as if she'd lost her mind. 'I'm not...'

'I ask little of you,' Maud boomed. 'But I'm asking this. You will support her.'

'She's making money from that damned photo.'

'She is, and it's magnificent. Have you seen the papers?'

'Yes.'

'Past the headlines?'

'No, I...'

'Then you don't know anything about it,' Maud boomed, and Harold quietly fetched a paper.

'You should read it.' Harold was in his seventies, mild-mannered and smart. 'It pays to do your groundwork, son,' he said softly. 'Especially when you're dealing with your grandmother. How about I take the ladies for drinks while you read? We'll see you in ten minutes.'

'I...'

'Ten minutes, son,' Harold said heavily. 'I doubt I can hold Maud for longer.'

* * *

He read the article in less than two minutes. He stood for another two, stunned.

Pyjama Girl Fund-raiser sold out—forced to shift to larger venue.

Public curiosity over the identity of the young woman seen travelling on the Ghan *with Australia's most eligible bachelor, Major Hugo Thurston, has reached fever pitch. Her identity has been established as Amy Cotton, retired dancer with the Australia Ballet. Public interest in the reclusive billionaire means rumours continue to fly.*

Darwin Special School's annual fund-raising concert normally fails to attract community interest, or indeed community support, and there has been talk of the school's closure. However, it now has interest in spades.

PJ, as the media is calling her, has agreed to dance with Darwin's disadvantaged children tonight, and Dame Maud Thurston confirms the Thurston family will be attending. The concert has thus become a must-be-seen-at event in Darwin's social calendar. Tickets are said to be selling for over a hundred dol-

lars and this small event looks like setting the Special School up for years.

PJ. Amy. What the…?

He looked up to find Maud watching him.

'She's not the same as your mother,' she said softly into the stillness. 'There's nothing in this for her.'

'Publicity…' He was still feeling stunned.

'She knows the Pyjama Girl thing is a one week wonder, so she's using it while she has it, to do some good. Come with us, Hugo. You need to see.'

He stared at his grandmother and she gazed back at him, calmly waiting. For him to see sense?

'This is not publicity for her,' she said. 'Amy is not like a single one of your father's girlfriends and it's about time you had the sense to admit it.'

She wasn't like those women. He knew it. But to pull her in…

He glanced at the paper. She was pulling herself in.

'Maybe…' he said.

'Yes,' said Maud. 'Definitely maybe. But if it's only maybe, shouldn't you be finding out for sure?'

* * *

'A thousand people!'

Amy had spent the last half hour calming over-excited kids, but now, two minutes before the curtain rose, she found time to clutch Rachel and quake. 'What was I thinking?'

'To help your school,' Rachel said.

That's right, Amy thought, fighting for calm. That was all she was doing. Supporting a school that made a difference.

She'd arrived for her job a week ago and had promptly fallen in love with what this school and its staff were doing for kids from dysfunctional backgrounds. But the press had been searching for her. Photographs had circulated and she and Rachel had been recognised and named.

The rest of the staff had quickly figured out her identity, but here, in this environment where everyone was working for needy kids, hype had no place. She'd given her new workmates a brief explanation. They'd laughed and teased her, but everyone agreed the fuss would die down in a week or so. They'd keep her presence here quiet. Meanwhile she'd thrown her energy into organising the kids' annual concert. It needed energy. It needed…something.

'Our concert's tiny,' the principal had told her. 'The kids perform for their parents and friends, but with our kids we often don't even get one adult per kid. We'd love it to be a fund-raiser but there's not much chance of that. If we could only get the publicity you're getting...'

She'd winced and agreed. And then next morning the local paper had run the headline again: *'Where's PJ?'*

This was starting to seriously bug her.

At her new local supermarket, she'd seen the notice the kids had put up, advertising their school concert. Someone had half covered it with an advertisement for a used car.

She'd readjusted the ad and she'd seethed. Here she was, getting publicity, when kids who needed it got nothing.

And then she'd thought... She'd thought...

Why not?

Hugo would hate it, she'd thought, horrified at herself for even thinking it. But the idea wouldn't go away.

The more she thought of it, the more she thought: do it.

It'd be nothing to do with Hugo, she'd told herself, breathless at mind plans that refused to be ignored. Surely all this fuss had to be good for something. And surely what she did was none of Hugo's business. After all, *she* was the one who'd been caught in pyjamas. What harm in using that short connection for good?

She thought, if she believed in this school…why not put personal dignity aside?

So she did.

And then the thing had snowballed. One of the teachers had a friend who knew how to wrangle the media. He'd come on board, and a thousand tickets later…

A thousand tickets!

Now it was time to perform.

'I just met your principal,' Rachel said, sounding awed. 'She has dollar signs coming out of her ears and she can't stop beaming. So go on, Ames. Get out there and wow them.'

'The kids…' She turned to see how they were coping.

'That's who you're doing this for,' Rachel said stoutly. 'Don't think of Hugo, or of two thousand eyes. You danced for more at the ballet and this is seriously awesome. Go for it.'

* * *

He was sitting in a school concert. He hadn't been at a school concert since he'd attended his own.

This was a very different school to the one he'd attended.

The kids were wobbly. They were strongly supported by the staff but each act was clearly an act of heroism. A kid with a guitar, strumming a simple tune, making a few mistakes but getting there. A group of twelve-year-olds doing handstands. A choir, slightly off-key, slightly behind the beat.

Maud had handed him the blurb on the school. It was for kids who'd found normal school too hard, or who'd played truant for too long and been left far behind, or for kids who'd been in trouble with the law and been referred here.

Troubled kids.

Would it have been better if there'd only been a few parents and friends to see them? he wondered, but he listened to the wave of applause after each act, he watched the glow as he saw each kid realise they were playing to a vast audience and he thought this would stay with them for ever.

This wasn't a critical audience. Everyone knew what this school was and they were in the mood to be pleased.

They were waiting to see PJ.

And word had flown that he was here as well. Necks were craned as people tried to see him, tried to see Maud, but at every new act their attention went back to the stage.

They were waiting—and so was he.

And here she was. Amy.

She bounced onto stage with a group of straggly adolescent boys, all dressed in martial arts uniform. They bounced around doing simple Tae Kwon Do moves, just enough to show that they were learning a little and aching to do more.

She kicked and punched at each kid and they blocked her with ease.

A couple of them threw her, and she let herself be thrown. She bounced up, beaming, bowing to the boys, bowing to the audience and the audience went nuts.

He watched her and felt…felt…

He didn't know what he felt, and she was gone. He forced himself to be still and watch on.

There were a few more acts. A girl with a glorious voice who brought the house down. A group of staff members with a comedy skit. A hip hop band and a malnourished kid who hip hopped like magic.

They were great. They were wonderful, but…

She was back, and again she wasn't alone. She was in the midst of six girls, adolescents of all shapes and sizes. The girls were dressed in black leotards. They swept onto the stage in true ballet style, using simple movements but choreographed to look elegant and sophisticated.

But elegant and sophisticated didn't begin to describe Amy. She was in the middle of the line-up—and she was wearing her pink satin pyjamas.

She was beaming from ear to ear.

The girls danced, simple steps, keeping in tune and in line.

Amy tried to keep up with them. She couldn't.

She was the clown, the klutz, trying desperately to keep up, flailing to spin, spinning too far, falling over, trying again.

The girls were trying not to giggle as they danced on. They weren't succeeding, but they kept in rhythm and they kept in line.

Amy kept on, valiantly trying to keep up with them. The moves she made were complex, he realised. This was clumsiness at its most skilful.

The girls spun. Amy spun, too, but she couldn't stop. She whirled out of control and wobbled and a couple of girls grabbed her and steadied her back into line.

The girls swooped and turned and Amy swooped with them—and fell and spun on her stomach. She rolled onto her back and gazed up at them and tried to figure how they were holding their hands. She tried to spin where she was.

She was a dancing Charlie Chaplin. She was totally, absolutely adorable.

The audience was rocking with laughter, loving her, loving the kids as they tried to keep her in line, loving the whole thing.

Hugo was just loving her.

How could he not?

They all loved her, he thought. The kids around her were misfits of adolescents who'd known Amy less than a week but already she had them in the palm of her hand. Already they knew simple dance steps. Who knew what she'd do with them, given time?

He'd thought before this: what a waste that she'd walked away from her ballet. But she hadn't. Ballet was a part of her. She was sharing that part.

'There's a girl who knows how to handle media attention,' Maud whispered, chuckling and chuckling. 'Oh, Hugo, isn't she wonderful? If you could learn to handle the media like this...'

'I can't dance,' he said faintly.

'You have your own skills.' She took his hand and held.

He glanced down at his grandmother's hand, wrinkled and gnarled. She expected a lot of him, he thought. She asked a lot.

But she and his grandfather had given him more.

He looked back at Amy and he thought: she's been forced to leave something behind—her life with ballet. But she was embracing this new life. She was using everything in her power to make it as good as it got.

If Amy could do this with what she'd been handed...what could he do with what he had?

The dance ended. The audience was on its feet, cheering wildly. Hugo was on his feet, too.

So much for solitude, he thought. It's not what it's made out to be.

He stepped out into the aisle and strode towards the stage.

People saw him and hushed. Maybe this was why they'd come. Maybe this was what they'd hoped for.

Amy couldn't see what was happening offstage. She was blinded by the lights. She turned and started ushering her girls offstage.

'Wait,' Hugo called, and she froze.

Her girls waited, and she had no choice but to wait, too. She stood, surrounded by her ballerinas, an adorable pyjama-clad nymph.

'Amy.'

He said her name out loud and she turned as if in a dream. Then she started looking...apprehensive?

What was she thinking? That he'd yell at her for using Thurston-fed publicity for her own ends?

He strode up the stage steps and reached her and the look on her face was unbearable. Despite the audience, the stage lights, the troupe of kid ballerinas, he held her shoulders—and he kissed her.

This was no kiss of passion. It was a firm, solid kiss of pride and claim and deep, primeval right. This was Amy. This was his woman.

'I'm so proud of you I'm almost tempted to get into a leotard and join you,' he said, and realised the microphones were sensitive and every sound on stage carried straight to the audience.

Amy smiled, tentatively, though, still unsure. But she was on stage, she had herself under control and she was more aware of the audience than he was.

'Thank you, Major Thurston,' she said simply. 'Your support means a lot to us, to this school, to these kids.' Then she turned to the audience. 'Thank you all so much for coming tonight. Your attendance money is wonderful, but we need more. These kids are capable of magnificent things— they just need belief. If any of you would like to donate, we have collectors in the foyer as you leave.'

There was a rumble of approval, but Hugo wasn't listening.

These kids are capable of magnificent things— they just need belief.

Amy was capable of magnificence without belief.

He thought of the moment at the railway station when he'd walked away. He'd thought he was protecting her by leaving her alone.

This woman was more than capable of protecting herself. She'd shown that time and time again. She did what she had to do, and she did it with courage and with honour.

And she'd given herself to him, and he'd walked away.

But now wasn't the time to say these things. The kids were starting to look uncomfortable. They'd been under the spotlight for long enough, and who knew more than him that spotlights eventually made you melt?

Amy had said what she needed to say. He should do the same and get off the stage.

Do it.

He grinned at Amy and he took her hand, turning them to the audience as a couple.

'Maybe now's a good time to make an announcement,' he said. 'I've handed in my resignation to the military and from now I'm taking on the reins of Thurston Holdings. It's a corporation I can be proud of, that you can be proud of. My grandfather ran it with Dame Maud by his side. Now, with similar support, with a similar woman, I hope I can do the same.'

There was a general gasp. Flashlights were firing from every angle.

Amy had stilled. He glanced at her and saw her face had lost its colour. He smiled at her. It was all he could do and for now it had to be enough. His hand tightened on hers and he saw some of the colour return.

'This school, these staff, are magnificent,' he told the audience, 'as Miss Cotton is magnificent. But now it's your turn. I'd like each and every one of you to get behind this place. Donate on the way out and, for every dollar you donate, Thurston Holdings will match it tenfold. We'll announce the total in the papers tomorrow. Let's see how much of a difference we can make, ladies and gentlemen.'

And then, to the sounds of exclamations and laughter, he turned and caught Amy into his arms. He hugged her hard and then motioned to the girls to precede them offstage.

'Now, if you'll excuse us,' he said to the audience, to laughter, to approval, to media frenzy, 'I've been in the desert for almost a week, and that's long enough for a man to be separated from the woman he loves.'

CHAPTER TWELVE

THREE days later, on a warm Saturday afternoon, they stood on Darwin Wharf and watched Maud and Rachel depart on what was billed as the cruise of a lifetime. Two weeks exploring the magnificent Kimberley coast. The women stood on the deck and beamed until they were out of sight.

When Hugo had broached the idea with Maud, she'd been delighted.

'Would you be sad if Rachel replaced me as your travel companion? She has another three weeks before she starts her new job. Amy's already started work, and I need to stay, too. There are so many company threads to pick up…'

'You'll stay here in Darwin? With Amy?' Maud's enthusiasm had bubbled. 'That's a wonderful idea. Rachel will love it, and we'll love it even more as we think about you two.'

'Maud…'

'Don't tell me. You're taking things slowly.' She'd chuckled. 'After kissing the lady in front of half of Darwin? After telling the world you love her? If that's slow, I'd hate to see fast.'

Fast…

Hugo stood beside Amy and thought of his plan and thought don't let it be too fast.

The boat had disappeared. Amy's eyes were misting. 'This is fantastic,' she whispered. 'Rachel will love it. She'll see so many rocks.'

'Maud might even come home knowing the history of granite,' he said, but he wasn't thinking of Rachel. He was thinking how beautiful this woman was. She was simply dressed, in an oversized white blouse and her customary leggings. Her hair was flying free. She was hugging Buster and he thought…things couldn't move fast enough.

'I'm glad Rachel rethought stowing Buster away again,' he said and she chuckled.

'Not likely. She gets rocks and I get Buster.'

'And you get me?'

She looked up at him, her smile fading a little. She was still unsure, he thought. She was still uncertain where their future would take them.

So was he, but he was sure of one thing. Where this woman went, he'd follow.

'We have tonight and tomorrow to ourselves,'

he said, turning prosaic. 'Would you like to do something together?'

'I...'

'Maybe dinner with an overnight stay somewhere special?'

She took a deep breath. 'Can Buster come?'

'Of course. Oh, and I have a gift for him.' He held out his hand to her.

She smiled and slid her hand into his and it felt as if it belonged there. He led her back to the car, hauled open the boot and produced a bag.

It was a small weekender made of soft cream leather, lined with sheepskin and with netting inserted at each end. *B Cotton Esquire* was elegantly tooled into the outside leather.

She giggled. Her giggle was gorgeous and he wanted to sweep her off her feet right now. But he'd waited for two days. He could force himself to wait a while longer.

'I didn't fancy you carrying that purse,' he told her, trying to sound prosaic. 'Not this weekend.'

'Are we going somewhere I'll need fancy luggage?' She looked doubtfully at the bag.

'Absolutely.'

'Will I need to dress up?'

'Yes.'

'Hugo, I'm not very good at…fancy.'

'Neither am I,' he said. 'This is a learning curve for both of us. Will you come with me?'

She hesitated for all of two seconds. She met his gaze, calm, clear, a woman knowing what she wanted, no matter what it took.

'Yes,' she said. 'I'll come with you. Wherever you take me, I'll go.'

He took her back to her apartment and she put on her nicest dress, the one she saved for post-season parties.

Where was he taking her? Some five-star hotel? A resort?

No matter. Yes, she was out of her comfort zone but she refused to be intimidated. This was Hugo, her lovely, war-worn warrior, tough as nails on the outside but with an inside of putty.

He'd left her for half an hour to prepare. She and Rachel were sharing a dead plain one-bedroom apartment on the outskirts of Darwin. Hugo was staying in one of the most expensive homes in the city.

Five stars. Different worlds.

But you can do this, she told herself as she heard

his knock. Buster was going wild with excitement. Buster loved this man, and so did she.

She opened the door and he was in evening dress. Deep black suit, crisp white shirt, black tie.

Five stars? Make it a hundred.

To her amazement, he took her to the airport. To a helicopter. She'd never been in a helicopter in her life. He guided her across the tarmac and she felt...weird.

He helped her in, organised her headphones, belted her in, and she had visions of the movie *Pretty Woman*.

She was being whisked off to the opera? From Darwin?

How far could a helicopter fly?

Hugo was climbing in beside her—*behind the controls. He flew these things?*

She couldn't help herself. A squeak came out all by itself.

'I'm trustworthy,' he said, smiling across at her. 'And I've practised a lot. I even took her up this morning for a trial run.'

He flew helicopters?

'Just sit back and enjoy it,' he said as he belted

himself in. 'I've told Buster not to worry. He's agreed. If Buster has courage, so should you.'

They flew for an hour, across some of the wildest country Amy had ever seen. 'This is the Kimberley,' Hugo told her as they followed great chasms of riverbeds, where water tumbled across rock formations that left her awed to silence.

'It's the end of an amazing wet season,' he told her. 'The country's at its best.'

The chopper was sweeping into the gullies, along riverbeds, over vast crags, plateaus, places she'd never dreamed could exist.

In one of the few moments she could spare from the scenery she glanced dubiously at the silk dress she was wearing—and the stilettos. Somewhere here…a resort?

What sort of resort was out here?

Where was he taking her?

And then the chopper started descending. Hugo was heading for a rocky plateau at the head of the most magnificent waterfall she'd ever seen. Three rivers merged to tumble from one plateau to the next, forming one vast wall of water.

On the plateau were three clearly delineated flows. The rest was low foliage, flat rocks and a myriad of waterholes. Sunlight was glistening on the water, crystal-clear.

'Did I tell you to bring your swimmers?' Hugo asked.

'No.'

'Really,' he said and grinned. 'That's a problem. Maybe you should just paddle.'

She looked down at the glistening water and thought: in your dreams I'll paddle.

'I brought my pyjamas,' she said stoutly. 'I'll wear them.'

'Then what'll you sleep in?'

Silence. His smile widened.

The chopper was growing closer to the plateau. There was something white...

A canopy. A table. Chairs.

A dog basket?

They dropped lower. She saw a bed under the canopy.

The table was set with white linen and silver cutlery.

Dinner in the wilderness?

'I...I thought you wanted me to dress up,' she breathed. 'And you've worn your dinner suit...'

'You think this setting doesn't deserve our best?'

'I…'

'It deserves my best,' Hugo said softly. 'You deserve my best.'

'We…' She was having trouble getting her voice to work. 'We could have just gone out to dinner in Darwin.'

'But we couldn't go swimming in Darwin,' Hugo said. 'Beware crocodiles.'

'There aren't crocodiles here?'

'Too high,' he said with satisfaction. 'Too far from the sea. And you need native permission to come in here, and no crocodile's been given permission. No one's been given permission—except us.'

She didn't speak. She couldn't speak. They landed. He led her to the table and seated her.

'Dinner is served, my love,' he said, and it was.

He said he'd done a practice run but it must have been more than simple practice. He had coolers of everything they could possibly want. More.

He produced tiny bread rolls with butter curls, salad, oysters and crayfish and a lemon mayonnaise that made the cray taste as if she must surely have died and gone to heaven. The chocolate mousse that followed made her sure of it. Cherries, strawberries, the best champagne…

Fillet steak for Buster, who'd pretty much decided this was where he wanted to stay for the rest of his life.

'If you're trying to seduce me,' she said cautiously as she polished off the last strawberry, 'I might as well tell you now that you've succeeded.'

'There's more to come,' he said but she rose and backed away from the table. This was over the top. Fabulous, amazing—scary.

'I…I'd like a swim,' she managed.

'In your pyjamas?'

'Maybe not,' she managed. 'Maybe I'll need them tonight.'

She turned her back on him and headed for the nearest waterhole—vast, deep, as big as a council pool. She slipped off her dress and dived in.

The water was cool and clear. She put her head down and swam, needing the cool and the clear, needing space to make herself think this was real.

He was how many stars?

This wasn't her world.

For the last couple of days she'd known Hugo loved her. The world knew Hugo loved her. She hadn't got her head around it—that he wanted her. And now…this night, this setting, made it more dreamlike.

More impossible to be real.

She swam.

Hugo swam as well, but he swam well away from her. Maybe he'd sensed her need for space.

It was antisocial, she conceded, the type of swimming she was doing, but the alternative… getting out and taking the next step…

This was a vast, expensive, glorious set-up. She should sink into it like a movie star. Bring on the paparazzi—this should be in the magazines.

It wasn't her.

She was scared. She shouldn't be. She loved this man but yet… Yes, she was scared. She blocked Hugo out of her mind as best she could, and she swam.

Hugo was done with swimming first. Dressed again in his dinner suit, he brought towels to the water's edge for her.

'Enough,' he said gently. 'I've frightened you.'

'You haven't,' she lied. She reached the edge and he tugged her up. He kissed her gently on the nose, then towelled her dry.

The sensation was incredible. Gentle, strong, warm. Sexier than anything she'd ever known.

She shivered and his arms came around her.

'Do you want to go home?'

After all this set-up…he'd take her home?

'N…no.'

He smiled and held out her dress.

'Respectability, my love.'

'Hugo, I don't belong here.'

'Neither of us do,' he said. 'Even if there's no crocodiles, it gets pretty inhospitable up here.'

'That's not what I meant. It's just…'

'Knowing where you belong? I have that problem, too. It's just…tonight I needed to have you all on my own. I wanted somewhere special, away from cameras, and this seemed perfect. Amy, I have a suggestion. You want to get dressed and see?'

She did. She still felt as if she was in some dream world where the lights would suddenly go on and the movie would be over, but Hugo was waiting to zip her dress. He stood looking like a hunk and a half, arms full of towels, Buster sniffing his feet.

He was real.

'Come and see,' he said softly, and he led her across to the canopy. Here was the bed—crisp linen sheets, fleecy blankets, mounds of pillows. No rough swag this.

'How did you get this stuff here?' she demanded and he grinned.

'I needed the chopper practice.'

'And if I hadn't said I'd come with you?'

'I'd have brought Harold and Margaret,' he said and she choked.

'For romance…'

'Ah, but you don't know if it is romance,' he said softly. 'You think you do. I can tell. You're looking at this and any minute now you expect to see a plane fly over dragging a great big sign saying, "Amy, will you marry me?"'

It was so much what she was thinking that she gasped.

'I'm not that corny,' he said softly and then glanced at the linen and silverware and grinned. 'I admit I'm pretty corny but not that corny. Amy, you have three gifts to unwrap.'

He stooped and felt under the mattress, hauling out three packages.

Three book-sized packages, wrapped in green tissue and white ribbon. Nary a diamond in sight, she thought, and was, stupidly, relieved.

'The first time I saw you, you were reading a book,' he said. 'Here are more.'

'I know everything I ever wanted to know about granite already,' she managed and he grinned.

'Are you sure? Open them.'

So she sat on the amazing bed, under the canopy, in one of the most amazing places in the world. And she opened her gifts.

Yes, they were books. She opened the first, and her grandmother's name was embossed on the front cover.

She gasped. What…?

'Look inside.'

She looked.

It was her grandmother's story. Her grandmother's people. The Arrernte.

It wasn't a story of here, of now, or even of her grandmother's time. It was the dream time story of the Arrernte, the native people who'd lived forever around the place Bess had called home. It was the stories of the great shadows of Uluru and Kata Tjuta. It was the stories that had been passed from generation to generation, of the land and the spirits. It was the story of a people.

She flicked the pages and her grandmother's words, the stories she'd passed down to Amy and to Rachel all those years before, sprang to life. Here they were, set down on pages and grown into more than Bess had ever told them, a story of dreaming and land and of life.

Amy looked up in wonder. 'Oh, my... Where did you...?'

'One of the men I worked with last week is of the Arrernte. He knew where I could find this.' He smiled. 'I'd have liked to have found the same for your spud farmer relatives, but that's a bit harder to come by.'

She flashed him a look of wonder, managed an awed smile and went back to reading. 'Grandma would have loved this,' she breathed.

And then she paused, thinking: no. Bess hadn't needed it. Bess had had it inside her. The things in this book—they'd belonged to her. She'd tried to pass it on, but she'd run out of time.

Amy had it in her hands.

These stories belonged to her.

'This is written by men and women of the Arrernte,' Hugo said softly. 'It's been told by story for thousands of years, but now they've put it in print, for you and for Rachel and for all those like you who need to reconnect. But your story is more.'

And he handed her the second book.

She opened it soundlessly.

It had the same cover, but this time her name and Rachel's were on the cover. And Buster's.

She flicked it open.

Here was her photograph as a baby. And Rachel's. Photograph after photograph. There were things like school sports certificates, photographed and set into the pages. School prizes. Tae Kwon Do awards.

The funeral notice for her grandmother. A picture of a grave.

She flicked on. Foster parents. Pictures. Names. Faces. Graduation pictures. Ballet...

'Rachel...' she started, trying to get her breath back. Trying to figure how he'd done this thing.

'Has helped,' he admitted. 'It's lucky she hasn't started work yet. I told her working on this was the cost of her fare on the boat. We had three days and we made a copy for her, too.'

'But how...?'

'We worked hard,' he said and tried to look modest.

She felt like laughing, but she didn't. She couldn't. 'Oh, Hugo...'

'This is you and Rachel belonging,' he said. 'Your story and Rachel's story. But there's more. At least, I hope there's more.'

One more package. She looked wonderingly into his face—and opened it.

The same type of cover.

Two names.

Amy and *Hugo*. No family names. Nothing but *Amy* and *Hugo*.

She flicked the book open to the first page. Here was the first photograph that had been taken of them together. The picture of them on the train.

A man about to kiss a woman.

There was something bulky between the next two pages.

She'd forgotten about breathing. Breathing wasn't important. There was only here. Only now. Only what lay between these pages.

She turned the page over and there it was, taped to the blank page, as all the rest of the pages were blank.

A ring.

She stared down at it. She'd thought… she'd thought…

No, she hadn't thought. She hadn't believed this could be real.

He'd taped it in place. Now he untaped it and held it out to her.

'Apart from that one kiss, our book's empty,'

he said softly. 'Our story's untold. But I believe we belong. I believe this story is our place in the world. If you accept this ring, we might write it together?'

She was having trouble seeing.

She didn't cry. She never cried. He held out the ring and she swiped back tears and made herself look.

A band of white gold. A single diamond. Tiny pink crystals set into the band and slightly larger ones set on either side of the diamond.

'They're pink felspar crystals,' he said, and unbelievably her warrior was sounding nervous. 'It's not…not the most expensive of rocks but… it seems…sort of ours? If you'll wear it.'

Ours.

She looked back down at the book. *Amy* and *Hugo*.

She gazed at the ring and then she gazed up at him.

He looked…scared she'd say no?

And gently, wondrously, magically, things fell into place.

No matter that he'd brought her to this over the top place to propose. No matter that he commanded a fortune, that he was a warrior who walked alone, that where this man walked the attention of the world went, too. This was Hugo. The Hugo of the book, Amy and Hugo.

Her Hugo. The man who'd share the rest of her life.

Her home.

He took her hands in his. He drew her to him and he kissed her.

'Amy Cotton,' he said, and the nerves had suddenly gone. Maybe he, too, sensed the inevitability of this moment, for his voice was steady, strong and loving. 'I know you don't wear tweeds,' he said. 'You haven't a moustache and as far as I know, you've never grown a turnip. Yet, despite all those drawbacks... Amy, I love you with all my heart. Will you marry me?'

And what was a girl to say to that?

There was no choice. This was her Hugo. Her life and her love.

She took his face in her hands, she drew him to her and she kissed him. She claimed him. Her man.

Would she marry him? How could she not?

From this moment forth, she was already married.

'Why, yes, Major Hugo Thurston,' she whispered. 'Why, yes, my dearest love, I believe I will.' She took a deep breath and she faced her future with conviction and with joy. 'I believe our story's waiting to be written. I believe we belong.'

* * * * *

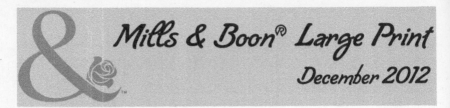

Mills & Boon® Large Print
December 2012

CONTRACT WITH CONSEQUENCES
Miranda Lee

THE SHEIKH'S LAST GAMBLE
Trish Morey

THE MAN SHE SHOULDN'T CRAVE
Lucy Ellis

THE GIRL HE'D OVERLOOKED
Cathy Williams

MR RIGHT, NEXT DOOR!
Barbara Wallace

THE COWBOY COMES HOME
Patricia Thayer

THE RANCHER'S HOUSEKEEPER
Rebecca Winters

HER OUTBACK RESCUER
Marion Lennox

A TAINTED BEAUTY
Sharon Kendrick

ONE NIGHT WITH THE ENEMY
Abby Green

THE DANGEROUS JACOB WILDE
Sandra Marton

Mills & Boon® Large Print
January 2013